ALPHA PROTECTOR DRAGON

LEELA ASH
TABITHA ST. GEORGE

CONTENTS

CHAPTER 1

Casey Briggs waited. He sat on stone, the backbone of Mother Earth, so that she might keep him strong. Dressed in her colors – black shirt, black pants, black tie – he summoned the mantle of her eternal patience, bidding it to settle his agitated heart. Beneath those clothes, hidden to human eyes but not those of the spirits, tattoos covered his arms. Proclaiming his ancestry and his nature in swirling black patterns that would last forever. Or at least as long as his body. Above him, Father Sun burned down, fierce in the desert morning. The shrill cry of a hawk echoed through the still air.

A good omen. The spirits guarded him in this treacherous time.

And so, he waited.

Mirages writhed and twisted at the horizon. From those shimmering lights, a figure emerged. A man, trudging slowly down the remains of an old road. Nearer he came, growing larger, more imposing, with each step.

Casey waited. Today was a momentous day, and the first

of its great challenges approached. He would not succumb to eagerness or impatience like some Shifter child.

At last, the stranger stood before him. He was an intimidating man, with short-cropped blonde hair and a scattering of scars. His spirit animal, a great white Dragon, loomed large, its battered maw crisscrossed with scars.

Casey wasn't daunted. His own spirit might be smaller, a lithe black Dragon with the curving horns that marked his Flight. But he knew he was the equal of any Shifter, and today, the spirits blessed him.

The stranger nodded pleasantly. "You must be Casey Briggs, from the Snow Flight."

"Flight of the Snows," he corrected him.

"Right. Finn Donnelly, First Flight."

The arrogance of that name was a slap that couldn't be ignored. "You are from Those Who Have Forgotten Themselves."

Donnelly's expression didn't change – though the icy scales of his Dragon suddenly blazed with a brilliant azure light. Anger. Good. Casey felt a surge of adrenaline as his own Dragon rose to that challenge and unfurled its great wings.

Yet, to give him credit, the white Dragon's words remained calm. "Is that what you call us? Let's stick to 'First Flight', okay? Little shorter than 'Flight of Those Who Can't Even Remember Why They're Here.'"

"Perhaps, 'The Forgetful Flight'?"

In the Spirit World, two Dragons locked eyes. The white rumbled its disapproval, a deep, bone-shaking growl. The black hissed back, its sinewy tail whipping from side to side. Casey felt its power sing through his blood, calling him to battle.

Until the big man shrugged. "Sure. What the hell. I've been called a lot worse."

The first spark of grudging respect lit in Casey's heart. A humble warrior was a dangerous opponent. One who could not be tricked into a foolish charge.

Calm, he ordered his Dragon. *Let us hear what this outsider wishes to say.*

"Why have you requested this meeting?"

Donnelly gazed out at the vast spread of emptiness that surrounded them. "Before I answer, can I ask one thing? Why did we have to meet at a rock in the middle of nowhere rather than, say, Starbucks?"

And just like that, irritation roiled the calm waters of Casey's soul. "Do you not know this 'rock'?"

The other Dragon scratched his nose. "Is it, uh, granite? Or something like that?"

"This 'rock'," he snapped, "is the Place of Meeting Outsiders. It is here that, in ages past, the Peoples of this land welcomed our Flight. When the Sand, Big River, and Sage Packs sought peace among themselves, they came here, and they bound their Packs by blood and marriage. This is a sacred place! There is no more auspicious site for a meeting!"

"Okay, well, I'm not from around here and I didn't know that," said the Forgetful idiot. "Look, I'm not trying to talk smack about your rock. I'm just saying that it's hot and I could really go for an iced latte right now. And Starbucks' seats are more comfortable," he added, as he swept a rock out from under himself.

How typical! Everything came down to indulgence and luxury for Those Who Have Forgotten Themselves. Were they even Dragons any longer – or just big, greedy lizards? "Again, I ask you," Casey said through gritted teeth, "why did you wish to speak to me?"

"Because my Flight has forgotten something," the big man said with a wide, guileless smile. One that made it hard to hold a grudge – even for a member of the proud Flight of the

Snows. "We're hoping you guys still remember it. You were at Fairburn's meeting, right?"

Rex Fairburn. Casey's lip twitched with disgust. The resorts that Bear built devoured the land and the silence with a hunger greater than any fallen Dragon's. When Fairburn put out a call, asking all the Shifters of the Southwest to come hear of a new 'danger', Miles Kennedy, the Alpha of the Flight of the Snows, ignored him. "He is a destroyer of tradition," he told his brothers of the Flight. "What threatens him does not threaten us."

Despite that, Casey *had* gone. The Bear was as blind and stupid as they come, yet no one could accuse him of failing his duties. He protected his people and his town with honor. That duty, that faithfulness, earned him the right of a hearing.

And what a hearing it was! The words spoken still burned their way through Casey's dreams. Oh, not Fairburn's worries about some new enemies, the 'Fangs of Apophis'. The Dragon neither knew nor cared about them. New enemies, old enemies… it was all the same. Those who remained vigilant didn't need to worry.

No, let the other Shifters fret about these Fangs. What had shaken Casey to the bottom of his soul was Finn Donnelly's announcement.

Wellsprings had returned. Founts of magic, they faded in ages past, leaving the world dull and mundane. Abandoning their protectors, the Dragons, to empty, meaningless existence. Now, the Wellsprings woke. Once more, Dragons were summoned to their most ancient duty: to protect the sacred waters that breathed life and wonder into the world. With magic's return, the Rite of Claiming was reborn. No longer would his Kind drift through the ages, alone. Fate's web grew strong again. Its touch, subtle and eternal, drew Dragons to their true Mates.

News like that should have sent Casey flying to the heavens, roaring his joy. Yet it was tempered with a bitter, terrible bile.

Fate had delivered the Wellsprings into the talons of Those Who Have Forgotten Themselves. They, not the Flight of the Snows, took up the most sacred duties. This Forgetful fool, Donnelly, who sat before him, pining for Starbucks? He had a *Mate*! That unworthy buffoon had somehow blundered through the Rite of Claiming and was bound to a woman in a sacred way that he, Casey Briggs, could only dream of.

The shame of that, the *unfairness*, drove him mad.

"So… the meeting?" Donnelly prodded. "Yes? No?"

That nudge yanked Casey out of his brooding, and he glowered at the cheery Dragon. "Yes. I went to the meeting."

"Good. So, you know about the Fangs. Well, we've been investigating this, and Fairburn found out that the Fangs are trying to summon some big, bad, demonic thing into this world."

Casey shrugged. Sounded about par for villains. They always hoped that spirits would just give them the power they were too lazy to build on their own.

"Does the name Nemagorix mean anything to you?"

At that, though, he straightened. "Yes. The Destroyer of Worlds. A creature from the spirit realms that is forever seeking to claw its way into this one."

"Awesome!" The outsider's smile blazed incandescent. "Score one for the smart Dragons! What can you tell me about Nemagorix?"

Like a poisonous serpent, worry crept into Casey's heart. No one could truly draw the Black Worm back into this world, could they? Especially not some band of outsiders. "Nemagorix is a great spirit. He has destroyed this world three times."

"Sorry?" Donnelly squinted at him. "If the world's been destroyed, why is it still here?"

"It isn't. This is a different world."

"Oh. So, when you say the world was destroyed, you mean bad stuff happened."

"No," Casey snapped as the tip of his Dragon's tail began to twitch with irritation. "I mean that the world died and a new one was born."

An important distinction – which the Forgetful One immediately waved off. "Sure. Let's not get bogged down over words. We both agreed this thing is bad. Apocalyptically bad. How did you guys stop him in the past?"

"We didn't. Nemagorix has not entered the world since we arrived. Only the People have faced him."

"Native tribes? Okay, how did they defeat him?"

Was this man not listening? "They didn't. He destroyed the world and when it shattered, he fell through the shards, back into the spirit realms."

"Huh," Donnelly said. "Well, I'm officially vetoing *that* plan for dealing with him."

"Once Nemagorix enters this world, all is lost. The only hope is to keep him at bay. Deny him a doorway."

"That's a better plan. How do we do that?"

"Er, prevent people from summoning him?"

"I kind of assumed that." A note of dry annoyance entered the Forgetful Dragon's voice. "Any specific advice you can offer? Like who summons him… how… where?"

"No. I can speak to my Flight, however. Some delve into history more than I do. They may be able to give insight."

"Thank you." The other man, of course, assumed they'd share that insight with Those Who Have Forgotten Themselves. Casey wasn't sure that was a good idea. "One last thing: have you heard of an Aye… uh, Ee-jee… No, dammit, I'm screwing this up. Hang on."

From his wallet, he pulled out a scrap of paper. One word was written on it, in a woman's delicate handwriting.

Aegis.

"Aegis," Casey replied.

"Ee-jiss." Donnelly muttered that a couple of times, committing the sound to his (limited) memory. "Do you know what the Aegis is?"

"No."

Immediately, his blue eyes narrowed with suspicion. "If you don't know what it is, how can you know how it's pronounced?"

"Because it's a Greek word. It means 'shield'. Why do you ask about it?"

"Nemagorix says that the Aegis needs to be destroyed before he can enter this world."

A critical secret – tossed out casually, as if it was of no worth. Casey fought to keep his shock off his face. *That* was the path his Flight should investigate. Surely, the People who made this Aegis would remember it.

Donnelly continued to frown, tapping a finger against his lips. "Why would a Native spirit use a Greek word?"

"For the same reason it calls itself Nemagorix. That's not a Native name either." As the Forgetful man's confusion deepened, Casey shook his head. "Nemagorix is a spirit. It's not 'of' this world or any of the world's people. It uses words it thinks mortals will understand."

"Then the person that spoke to it was smarter than me!" A fact that did not surprise Casey.

Words ceased, leaving nothing but the mutterings of Brother Wind. Each Dragon sat, lost in his own thoughts, until Donnelly stretched. "Well, thank you. I've learned a lot. Is there any information or help I can give your Flight?"

Oh yes, there was.

How?!? How did you find your Mate? Tell me everything about the Rite of Claiming! What does it feel like when your soul finds what it lost, the spirit that will make you whole again?

Not one of those questions passed his lips. Inconceivable that he should abase himself, show weakness, before a member of that arrogant 'First' Flight.

"No. Thank you," was all he said.

"Well, if you find out anything about Nemagorix or this Aegis, please let me know. We've had our differences in the past, but I think we can agree that neither of our Flights wants to see the world destroyed."

Casey made a noncommittal grunt. The Flight of the Snows didn't need Forgetful's 'help' to protect their lands.

Donnelly rose stiffly to his feet, brushing sand and gravel from his jeans. "I didn't see your car. Can I offer you a lift back to town?"

"No." As if a Dragon, a Prince of the Air, needed cars! "I am not finished here."

The outsider scanned the land about them. No doubt, he saw nothing except emptiness. "What needs doing? Can I lend a hand?"

"No." The very thought was amusing. "I need to thank the spirits of this stone for helping us hold a productive conversation. I should also honor the memories of those who've gone before us."

Of course, He Who Had Forgotten Himself didn't understand. "Sure. Uh, I'll leave you to settle up with your rock then. I'm gonna head back and get something cool to drink."

With that, he left, stomping away like some wingless animal. Agitation and confusion departed with him. Casey sighed with relief as peace settled over him once more.

The outsider had given him a great deal to think about. There was much to do.

And *his* Flight, not some 'First' Flight, would do it.

First, though, the day's second task awaited. One of far greater importance than the words of a strange Dragon.

CHAPTER 2

Any lost tourist who blundered into Ringo's Spread immediately turned tail and fled back to the safety of Route 491. Honestly, the place looked like the Trailer Park from Hell. Three dozen decrepit single-wides lay scattered about. Scores of dusty motorcycles and junked cars littered the scrub. Music – usually heavy metal – wafted through the air at all hours while a crowd of leather-clad men and women lounged, drinking beers.

To any civilized person, the whole place screamed 'DAN-GER!' Whoever those people were, whether drug dealers, smugglers, or plain old criminals, they were clearly up to no good.

But Lily King wasn't a civilized person. When she looked at Ringo's, she saw home. The Den of the Sand Pack, one of the great Wolf Packs of the Four Corners region.

She strode through a sea of familiar faces. Bone-Dog, Deadbeat, the White-Tail sisters. Even Ghost, shaded by a huge umbrella, glanced up from her computer and waved. The sight of her hunched over in her wheelchair, typing furi-ously, brought a grin to Lily's face. The girl was one of her favorite Packmates. Once, some lone Wolf had called her a 'gimp' and said she ought to be 'put out of her misery.' "What good is a Wolf that can't run?" he laughed.

Well, they'd made *him* run, driving him into the desert with bared fangs. Maybe Ghost wasn't like other Wolves. She ran through virtual fields and hunted electronic prey. But she was still a Wolf and the Sand Pack honored her. And that lone Wolf? He never showed his tail in these lands again.

"Hey, Lily! What's up?" Ghost called.

"No idea. Dad wants to see me." She paused, scooting under the edge of the other woman's shade. The Old Man had told her to come 'right away'… but it was good to make him wait a bit. Remind him that he might be an Alpha of this Pack, but his authority had limits. She was his equal, not his 'little girl.'

"Bet it's got something to do with his guest," Ghost whispered. "Dragon flew in about a half-hour ago. One of the Snow Flight."

"Flight of the Snows," Lily corrected her. They were a prickly bunch, stuffed from their horns to the tips of their tails with pride, protocol, and etiquette. Insult one and they'd sulk for *centuries*. Any normal Shifter would die long before that grudge did!

On second thought, maybe it wasn't so smart to make people sit around twiddling their thumbs. "Thanks for the heads up. I better get moving."

And maybe she ought to clean up a bit. She tossed her helmet down by Ghost's wheelchair and ran her fingers through her brown hair. Short curls crushed flat by the helmet's weight fluffed under her touch, surrounding her delicate, fine-boned face. A few swats dusted the worst of the grime off her riding leathers. "How do I look?"

"Like you've been dragged behind a car for a couple of miles," Ghost informed her.

"Bite me."

With a laugh, Ghost snapped at her. Lily flipped her friend the bird and hustled over to her father's trailer.

Air conditioning was for wimps, not Wolves, and so the trailer's innards burned like a furnace in the midday sun. The cheap curtains drawn tight over the windows didn't do anything to cool the place. They just made the furnace dark and gloomy.

As she adjusted to the shade, Aaron King spoke from somewhere in the shadows. "Lily. How nice of you to finally join us."

"I'm a Wolf, not a dog. If you wanted me to 'Heel!', 'Sit!', or 'Stay!' you should have trained me better."

Objects emerged from the darkness. Her father's couch, desk, and table (significantly cleaner than normal). King himself, glaring, hands on his hips, his long salt and pepper hair pulled back in a neat pony tail. Hell, he'd even waxed his mustache.

Wow. Lily snorted. Things must be serious.

The last figure to emerge from the gloom took her breath away.

He sat in the corner, as still as an adder. Shirt and shoes as black as midnight, covered by a black suit despite the heat. Hair like a raven's wings swept away from a narrow face. High cheek bones, full lips, a firm, pointed chin… his was the face of aristocracy. The fine-boned elegance that came from centuries of royal breeding. From his piercing gaze to the quiet, understated power of his lithe body, he radiated a simmering, fierce masculine aura. The edge of a tattoo peeked out beneath his cuffs. A hint that something wilder, more primal, lurked beneath his refinement.

Hot as hell – if you were into ominous and possibly malevolent Bad Boys.

Which Lily was.

Shimmering at the edge of her vision, she saw it.

His Dragon.

Shifters often saw the outlines of other Shifters' spirit animals. It was like having a second pair of eyes, one that saw the spirit lands and not the mundane world of men. Those 'eyes' opened now to reveal a towering creature, far larger than the shabby trailer. A Dragon crouched beside the stranger, fierce and proud. Like him, it was a creature of midnight. Black scales glittered. Long and slender, its serpentine body coiled tight. On its head it bore the pair of slender, backward-curving horns that marked it as a Dragon of the Flight of the Snows.

"I remember you," she told him. "You were at the meeting Rex Fairburn called. I don't remember your name though."

Her dad supplied that missing information. "This is Casey Briggs, a representative of the Flight of the Snows. Mr. Briggs, this is my daughter Lily."

He rose in one fluid, graceful motion and bowed his head in a formal greeting. "I bless the sun that shines upon our meeting, Ms. King, and pray that Brother Wind brings fortune to us both. The Sand Pack has been an ally of my Flight. May the day's journey tie our Kinds closer together."

Because 'Hi, nice to meet you' just isn't good enough for the Stick-Up-the-Butt Flight...

Her own spirit, a shaggy brown Wolf, pranced with excitement.

Play! it urged her. *Nip! Bite! Tease!*

No. Insult = century-long grudge, remember?

Her Wolf didn't see the problem with that.

But Lily did, and she held her tongue. "What's the occasion?"

"Not 'what.' *Who.*" Her father waved at the couch. "Please, have a seat."

Suspicious, she flopped down on the end farthest away

from their visitor. More carefully, the Dragon settled back into his chair. "This about those Fangs of Apophis that have Fairburn so wound up?"

"In a way, yes." Ignoring her, her father turned his chair toward Casey and leaned forward, grim and intent. "In the last six weeks, my daughter has been assaulted four times."

The hackles on her Wolf's neck rose and all thoughts of play evaporated. "What's that got to do with anything?" Lily muttered.

"You think the Fangs are responsible for this?" said the Dragon.

Like anyone here was stupid enough to miss that hint! "So what? If they come for me, it saves me the trouble of hunting them down."

She might as well have been talking to herself because both men ignored her. "I do, Mr. Briggs. The attacks are becoming more lethal too."

"Lethal my ass!" Lily howled. "A couple of cracked ribs never killed anyone!"

"Last Wednesday, a truck pulled up beside her at an inter-section and opened fire."

Before driving off, too fast for her to follow. That attack *was* annoying, she had to admit. SOBs had 'killed' her favorite bike.

The Dragon leaned forward too, hands steepled together. "Why would the Fangs – if they exist – want your daughter dead?"

"I have no idea," her father sighed. "We helped Fairburn destroy one of their safe houses. My first thought was that they wanted to punish me."

Because, of course, everything was always about him, not her. Lily considered drawing the .357 hidden under her jacket. Maybe if she put a few slugs through the trailer's roof the two men would remember she was here.

"Yet they haven't struck at Fairburn, so I can't believe that's their true goal. It's a mystery."

Lily glowered at the two, arms folded across her chest. Furious that they discussed her like she wasn't even in the room.

No one noticed. "You have a conundrum on your hands," Casey admitted, leaning forward. "Why share it with me, though?"

"Because of this."

From his pocket, her father drew a large golden coin. Thick and heavy, it oozed antiquity, like a Spanish *doubloon*. Strange letters had been clawed onto its surface, more like gouges than words.

A tremor rocked the Dragon. He rose, blood draining from his face. "Aaron King, son of Davis, son of Lawrence, son of Justice King, I stand before you."

What the hell? Lily edged away from the raving lunatic. Why was he rattling off her dad's family tree?

Her father held that coin up like a talisman and the Dragon continued his dazed speech. "I, Casey Briggs, Brother of the Flight of the Snows, thank you for the gift you gave the Marakeen. I will assume the debt and repay it, though it cost me my life's blood."

None of this made sense. Not the Coin of Dragon-Buying. Not the weird, formal speech. Heck, not even the words! What was a 'Marakeen', anyway?

Whatever it meant, that promise seemed to reassure her dad. "Thank you for honoring your Flight's debt." He placed the coin down gently on the coffee table.

Casey picked it up and held it, reverently, in his hands. "What would you have of us? Name this thing and I shall provide it, if it is within my power."

"I want you to protect my daughter."

Outrage coursed through her. Her Wolf scrambled to its feet, hackles rising.

But this was a 'guy thing', an agreement between the 'boys'… and no one so much as glanced her way. That insufferable Dragon simply bowed his head and rumbled, "I will guard your daughter, for all my life if need be, until the day you deem this threat vanquished."

"Like hell you will!" Lily barked.

Now they looked at her. Snow Snake seemed surprised by her fury – but her dad wasn't the least bit surprised.

"I don't need a babysitter, or a bodyguard, or whatever the hell you want to call this idiot."

"Lily!" Her father jerked his head at the scowling Dragon. "Remember your manners!"

Oh, hell no she wouldn't! Screw the Flight of the Snows and the threat of century-long pout-fests. "No. Veto. End of discussion. You don't get to assign me a protector like I'm five years old."

The insults were taking their toll on Casey's patience. His lips pinched and, in the shadows, his Dragon lashed its tail like a furious cat. "Aaron King is not only you father, he is your Alpha. You *owe* him obedience."

That was it. *That* was the last straw. Her Wolf exploded in sharp, furious barks as Lily rounded on him. "I'm an Alpha too and I do *not* obey anyone!"

"You're… an Alpha?" He blinked at her father. "Is your daughter from another Pack?"

"No!" Lily howled. "I am one of the Alphas of the Sand Pack! *This* Pack."

"'One' of the Alphas?" Like an affronted lord, the Dragon sneered at her. "What a foolish thing to say! There can only be one Alpha."

Three steps, and she was right in his face. Casey backed up but hit the chair and nearly toppled over. Teeth bared in a snarl, eyes blazing, she stared him down. Letting him know that – Dragon or no – she wasn't afraid of him.

"You don't know *anything* about Wolves! Our Packs have two Alphas. One for the women, one for the men. Normally, they're Mates, and they're equals. Maybe Dragons beat each other up until there's only one left standing, but we're Wolves. We work together. We're a Pack. And a Pack has *two* Alphas."

"A fact my *father*," she spat, "forgets."

"I haven't forgotten you're my daughter," he rumbled, anger simmering behind his words.

Lily rounded on him, abandoning the Dragon. "Well, you *should*! I am an Alpha – your *equal*! But you can't see that. No, to you I'll always be a 'daughter'. A little girl. Your 'princess.'"

"I never spoiled you!"

"You've never respected me either! You would *never* pull this on my mother!"

"YOUR MOTHER IS DEAD!" he roared, pushed to the breaking point by her rebellion. "And I will *not* lose you!"

Silence fell as the two Wolves glared at each other. Even the music outside had been turned off. The whole Pack listened, nervous, as their Alphas fought.

Lily was the first to turn away – but not in submission. "You lose a little bit of me every time you dishonor me. Today, you've lost a lot."

"Lily..."

Elbowing her way past him, she stormed out the door. Staring Wolves startled and quickly tried to hide the fact that they'd been eavesdropping.

Lily ignored them. She stalked to her motorcycle and snatched up her helmet.

Her father, it seemed, was content to let her go.

Her new bodyguard, however, was a different matter. He

banged out of the trailer behind her and stomped over. "Ms. King, we need to talk."

"No, we don't. *You* need to get lost. Fly back to your Lair in the Sierra Nevadas and sit on a pile of gold... or whatever it is Dragons do for fun."

In his spotless black suit and leather shoes, he was out of place in the shabby trailer park. Like a movie star wandering through a flea market. Yet he held onto the conversation with a tenacity that would impress any Wolf.

Or dog.

"My Flight owes your father a Blood Debt. Repaying it is the highest honor any Dragon could receive."

"How nice for you," she sneered, as she swung her leg over her Harley. "Too bad your 'honor' dishonors *me.*"

"You mustn't think of it that way. I'm a Dragon, the strongest of Shifter Kinds. You are... well, just a Wolf."

Just a Wolf? *Just*? Rage tinted the world red as the Harley came to life beneath her. "Oh, hey, that's a great argument. 'I'm not dishonoring you, you just suck!'"

"That isn't what I meant!"

"Well, it's what you said!" Damn, the sooner she escaped this pompous fool the better!

He suddenly seemed to notice the rumbling motorcycle. "Where are you going?"

"Away. I've got errands to run."

"Where?"

"None of your business." Ooh, it felt good to say that!

"Ms. King," he huffed, drawing himself up in indignation, "I am your bodyguard. I cannot guard you properly unless you tell me where you're going."

"Sucks to be you, then," she purred.

That felt even better. As did throwing the Harley in gear and leaving him standing in a cloud of dust.

This damned Wolf Princess was *not* making life easy!

Did she truly think that flight would make him abandon his duty! No, this was the greatest honor of his life. He summoned his Dragon, letting its power wash over him. Around him, the Wolves of the Sand Pack gaped, wide-eyed, as he Shifted. His body stretched into a sinuous, glittering serpent. Black wings like curtains of night burst from his shoulders. Gleaming ivory horns curled from his brow, the one bit of light in his Dragon's somber hues. With not a single glance at his bedazzled spectators, Casey launched himself into the air. Returning to the element that Dragons ruled.

It didn't take him long to catch up to Lily. No creature on Earth moved as swiftly as his Kind! And, oddly, the Wolf dawdled her way north on back roads, clearly in no hurry to finish her errands.

When she spotted him, she pulled off the side of the road and gazed upward. Casey hovered over her, patient. No doubt, she intended to rail at him. To try to drive him off with insults or pleas. Well, she would find him implacable. Her words would fall on deaf ears.

In fact, no words came. Scowling, Lily studied him. Then she grinned. A big, Wolfish grin. The smile of a playful imp with a nasty idea of fun.

Hopping back on her bike, she drove north. Faster this time. Casey had to push himself to keep up. Her plan quickly became clear: she made a beeline for the town of Cortez. A place full of mortals – who would panic the moment they saw him, a 'monster' out of legends. Among the Shifting Kinds, Bears and Wolves had it easy. A human who saw them Shifted was frightened, nothing more. But Shift in from of them – or Shift into something 'impossible' like a Dragon or a dog-sized Rat – and all hell broke loose. People panicked, screamed, fled. Their minds, so used to a 'normal', sensible world, buckled. They hallucinated, desperately trying to force the world to 'make sense' again.

If he flew into a large town, no telling how much harm he'd do.

Or, rather, how much damage *another* Dragon would do. If one of the 'First' Flight trailed her, then yes, Lily could dump them by sticking to populated areas. But the Flight of the Snows had not forgotten themselves. They remembered that Dragons were meant to be the Princes of the Air.

Softly, with deep, rumbling words, he called out to Brother Wind.

Brother, hear me! Heed the plea of the one you hold aloft. Wrap me in the fringes of your cloak. Hide me from the eyes of enemies and foolish ones.

Around him, motes of light danced through the air. He still saw perfectly, yet the next time Lily glanced up, she smiled in triumph at the 'empty' sky above her.

Casey smiled too, with a mouth full of fangs.

Two can play games, Princess!

At the edge of Cortez, she pulled up to a ratty food cart and ordered a burger and fries. As she devoured the greasy fare, he circled overhead. Riding the thermals like a giant hawk. Despite everything, he found himself admiring her. The delicate beauty of her sharp, elfin face. The sleek lines of her long legs and taut bottom, covered by a form-fitting leather that left nothing to the imagination.

Natural though they were, such thoughts disturbed him.

This is my ward, the woman I am sworn to guard. She is the daughter of an ally of the Flight. To lust after her is wrong. It is Incorrect Behavior, which angers the spirits of the land. I can no more touch her than I could touch my cousin.

If he had a cousin. Which he didn't. Mates had vanished when the magic of the Wellsprings drained out of this world. When that happened, most Dragons threw themselves into hook-ups and doomed marriages, unions where the wife was destined to age and die as her husband, eternally young, watched on in misery.

Not his Flight. Miles Kennedy, his Alpha, forbade false unions. When natural, masculine needs grew too great to bear, he and his brothers could seek release with prostitutes or women who would not mind if their lovers vanished in the morning, never to be seen again. But love? Marriage? No. It was forbidden, doomed. No marriage could withstand the weight of the years.

Though the Fools Who Had Forgotten Themselves swore they'd Claimed Mates. True Mates. And Wellsprings were returning to life, all across the world. Which meant...

Which means nothing. I don't love Lily King. I couldn't Claim her, even if I wanted. All I'm doing is staring at her ass – and that is profoundly disrespectful.

Movement drew his eye to the earth. Lily had finished her lunch and returned to her bike. Casey drifted after her, pleased with his stealth and cunning.

He expected her to wander into Cortez. Do some shopping or get a tune-up for her motorcycle. Instead, she headed over to Route 491. Traffic was heavy today and as she watched for an opening, he circled again.

When the break came, his clever plan fell to pieces.

Lily raised her gloved fist and waved a middle finger at the 'empty' sky above her. She might not know where he was – but she guessed he was there. With a howl like a wild boar, her motorcycle leaped onto the highway and charged off.

Casey threw himself after her. Great wings beat furiously, tearing through the hot air with every ounce of their strength.

But the bike pulled away, zipping around an SUV at an insane speed that made him want to scream in horror. Dammit! His ward was going to get herself killed trying to escape him!

Once the road ahead cleared, Lily opened the bike up and, with a cackle of delight, she sailed off into the distance.

Leaving him flapping impotently behind her.

Dragons might be the fastest Kind – but Harley-Davidson was faster. He knew an impossible race when he saw it, and so he banked and swept back toward Cortez.

Fifteen minutes and one rental car later, Casey was back on the road. Weaving through traffic, horn blaring, frantically trying to catch up to his runaway Princess.

By the time he found her, Lily was cruising along at a nice, steady 85 mph.

On an unstable, unprotected piece of metal that might tip over at any moment.

Bile rose in his throat. Yes, his ward seemed determined to kill herself. One slip and there'd be nothing left of her but a red streak on the highway.

He didn't know where she was going. Someplace far away – maybe Flagstaff or even Phoenix. But there was one thing

Casey Briggs *was* sure of: whenever Lily King reached her destination, he was going to pound that motorcycle into scrap metal. She could ride home with him or walk. He didn't care which.

The one blessing was that the Wolf didn't expect a car pursuit. He dropped to her speed a ways back and followed, scowling and furious.

Time passed. Route 491 turned into 160 and the odds of Flagstaff increased. The desert flowed by on both sides of the road, lulling him. A monotonous lullaby of gravel and stone.

When he spotted the first car, he thought nothing of it. An unremarkable black SUV with tinted glass, it slowly crept up on him. Eighty-five apparently wasn't fast enough for some people. Though, honestly, it was only ten miles over the speed limit out here.

It wasn't until the thing was right on his tail that the first alarms went off in his head. As it pulled out to pass him, he saw another black SUV behind it. And then another, and another. Four cars. All black, anonymous, and impossible to see into. One by one, they pulled over in perfect unison, like four metal dancers.

Government workers?

Or something more ominous? Maybe the Fangs that supposedly hunted his ward?

His gut screamed at him to attack. A twist of the wheel would send one, maybe two, careening off the road.

But what if they were innocent? A bunch of military or government workers, trying to get someplace, fast? That fear stayed his hand. Could he really kill these people on a whim? A hunch?

He couldn't. Instead, he flashed his headlights.

Lily caught that in her rearview mirror. Even this far back he saw the Wolf tense as she studied those approaching cars. She eased off the throttle and cruised, slowing quickly.

The little pack of SUVs broke up. Two sped ahead, blowing past Lily. A third pulled back into the right lane just beyond Casey while the fourth paced him in his blind spot.

The SUV ahead of him braked, unwilling to pass the slowing Wolf. A dim rage boiled to life in Casey's heart as he realized he'd made a mistake. Anyone in a hurry would have sped off into the distance.

These guys weren't trying to get anywhere. They were hunting.

All hesitation vanished. One fist punched the horn, blaring out a warning to Lily. With his other hand, he jerked the car to the left, cutting off his pacer.

At that sudden move, his enemies sprung their trap.

The lead SUV slammed its brakes, screeching to a halt. Beside it, its partner did the same.

Blocking off both lanes of the highway ahead of Lily.

Time seemed to slow, weighed down by his horror. The Wolf braked and swerved, but her momentum still sent her flying into the rear of a car.

With almost supernatural grace, she wrenched her bike sideways, swinging her leg over the seat as she did. It slammed into the back of the SUV, taking the brunt of the impact. The Wolf toppled off. Stunned, but with two uncrushed legs.

For the moment. But the third car sped up, intent on ramming her.

The Fangs of Apophis weren't trying to kidnap her, he realized.

They wanted her *dead.*

Something he would *not* allow.

Casey floored the gas and his sedan leaped forward. He yanked the wheel viciously to the right, plowing into the SUV's rear with enough force to jog its rear tire off the road.

Nature did the rest. The soft dirt at the edge of the road

gave way and the driver yanked his wheel, too hard. The SUV flipped, rolling off into the scrub. Bits of metal flew off as it bounced.

He had one moment to gloat – and then the last SUV rammed him. Bigger and heavier, it pitched his sedan into that treacherous sand too. Now he was flying through the air, the car spinning onto its side, sailing toward a crash that would kill any man.

But Casey wasn't just a man. He was a Dragon.

At the first impact, he set his Shifter soul free. Even as the sedan sailed through the air, twisting with deadly force, light filled it. Scales flashed across his skin, hard as a Kevlar vest. Claws lost their grip on the wheel and his body swelled, filling the car with its bulk. But as his body fought to escape that metal prison, the sedan slammed into the ground.

Torn by forces from inside and out, it exploded. Doors and roof flew off. As the car rolled wildly off into the sage, it left behind one thing: an enormous black Dragon.

Who was *seriously* ticked off.

On the road, doors flew open, spilling out a dozen men with automatic weapons. The groggy Wolf took one look at them and – thank the Spirits! – did the only sensible thing: she leaped into the drainage ditch and went belly to the ground as bullets whined through the air around her.

Around *his* ward! Around the woman *he* had sworn to protect!

A roar of pure fury erupted from his fanged maw. One sweep of his wings sent him soaring up. A dozen shocked faces followed him, and the villains turned their weapons upward. Bullets sprayed across his scales. Irritating, like a swarm of nipping insects.

Casey dropped from the sky, crushing the roof of the lead SUV. Then his head whipped to the side and breathed, sending a blast of fire searing into the second vehicle. Flames as hot as napalm slammed through its open doors, filling the inside with fiery death.

And just like that, the attack crumbled. Every surviving Fang bolted for the last car standing. Three made it inside – and the third yanked the door shut, abandoning the rest of his team. Another fiery breath silenced their shrieks of fear and the scorched SUV tore off, flames dribbling down its side.

Foes defeated, Casey rose on his hind legs and peered about. Where was Lily? Where was the only thing that truly mattered here?

Belly low to the ground, a brown Wolf peeked out of the ditch. Dragon and Wolf stared at each other for a moment, and then Casey Shifted, dropping back into human form.

Lily tiptoed out of hiding. He caught a glimpse of something around her neck. A braid of some sort, with a silver medallion. Then she, too, Shifted.

Hands on her hips, she surveyed the carnage around them. "Okay. I'm impressed."

Gratifying, but beside the point. "Are you all right?"

"Few cuts and scrapes. Maybe another cracked rib to add to the total but eh, I'll live."

Relief warred with annoyance. In the end, annoyance won. "*This* is why you need protection!"

Immediately, her lips curled back in a feral snarl. "I don't 'need' anything."

"Oh really? Without my warning, you'd be splattered across the back of that SUV!"

With a roll of her eyes, she stalked toward the front of the crushed vehicle. "I would have noticed them before they attacked."

"And then what?" he sneered. "How would you have dispatched four cars full of gunmen?"

She crouched to peer into the remains of the car he'd landed on. "Oh, yuck. No one alive in *that* pancake."

"Well?" He wasn't letting her off the hook that easily.

The burning SUV she wrote off with a single glance. "Nope. Nobody there either. Did you leave *anybody* alive to interrogate? I'd like to know why they're so hot to kill me."

She began to stroll past, toward the last SUV, which had come to rest, upside down, out in the scrub. But Casey blocked her path, fists planted on his hips. "Admit it. You need my protection."

"No, I don't."

"There's no way you could have defeated that many enemies!"

For once, neither anger nor challenge twisted Lily's face. Only a quiet, proud, defiance. "Maybe not. If I couldn't flee, I might have died. But I still don't 'need' anything. I accept my odds, my life, and my death."

"You're insane!"

"I'm a Wolf!" Her chin rose.

Spirits, there was no reasoning with this creature! Casey shook his head in disgust. "I'm starting to think those two are the same thing."

At his insult, she tossed her head back and laughed. "See? You're learning!"

It was an… enchanting sound. Laughter lit her face and set her green eyes on fire with a wild, fierce joy. A joy he knew well. It was the ecstasy of flying through a thunder cloud. The delirious glee that flooded your body in the middle of battle, when any mistake could bring your death.

He'd never seen that joy in a woman's face, and he felt a heat rise within him.

Stop. This is Incorrect Behavior. Remember that. To touch your ward is to dishonor her.

Unaware of the desires she stirred within him, Lily

scrambled across the drainage ditch. "Come on. Let's see if there are survivors out there."

The debris strewn across the desert didn't give him much hope. "And then?"

"Then I finish my errand."

Did he have to fight for every scrap of information? "Which is?"

"I want to talk to some Witch Hares in Sedona."

He was about to ask her reason – then suddenly realized he knew it. "Is it about your necklace? Clothes and jewelry Shift with us. I've never seen anything that didn't vanish."

A slight limp slowed her down. Casey caught up and walked beside her. "Yeah, it was a present from my mother. For years it was just a normal necklace. Then, about six months ago, it stopped Shifting with me. And it started doing some other weird crap." She waved her hand vaguely but didn't offer more details. "I've gotten curious enough that I want to talk to the Hares."

An idea he approved of. It might well explain why the Fangs hunted her.

For now, though, he kept his suspicions to himself.

CHAPTER 4

The thoroughly sucky day stayed true to the end. Only the SUV driver survived – and he shot himself as they walked up. Hours later, that still haunted Lily. He was a Bear, a big man with a sad, round face. Why would he kill himself rather than be questioned? Did the Fangs of Apophis truly hold Shifters' families hostage? Any Bear, no matter how fallen, would die for his family.

Her Harley still ran – if you could call 30 mph 'running'. She limped to the next town while Casey flew, invisible, overhead. Nice trick, that. They ended up renting a car. Which meant four hours of uncomfortable, boring silence with Mr. All Work No Play.

Then, in the perfect crappy ending to a miserable day, the Sedona Hares had no idea what her necklace was. Oh, they offered to keep it, and study it, and lock it away... if she wanted.

Hell no. It was hers. The only thing her mother left her other than her looks.

A full day wasted and nothing to show for it. Just before midnight, Casey booked them into the Mystical Desert motel. Two adjoining rooms full of fake Native pastel paintings and New Age drawings.

"I hate Sedona." She glowered at a poster of dolphins 'swimming' through the Milky Way surrounded by UFOs. "Why couldn't we push on to Flagstaff? At least it's not full of moonbats."

"You'll survive. A little fluff never killed anyone."

"You don't know that…," she muttered.

"Get some sleep. We'll head home early tomorrow."

He was setting schedules now? Planning her days? What was next? A leash and collar? She ought to call him on that nonsense, but he walked off before she could.

Just as well. She sighed as she peeled off her jacket. Until they got the Fangs off her case, she was stuck with him. After this attack there was no way she could persuade her dad to dismiss the Dragon.

The worst part? She couldn't even call Casey 'useless.' Today proved that. It had taken all her skill and strength to just stay alive. The fighting, *all* of it, fell to her unwelcome bodyguard.

Nope. Though it hurt to admit it, on her own she would have died.

Still didn't mean she was going to thank him, though. Pants and jacket tossed aside, she dragged her bruised body into bed and tried to ignore the sickly-sweet herbal scent that clung to its sheets.

In her dream, Lily stood atop a mountain. The desert stretched out beneath her while above a storm raged. Forks of lightning split the sky, though not a drop of rain fell. The air tickled her nose, rich with the scents of the south. *Piñon* and sage, crisp and clear.

Wind swirled around her, ruffling her short curls. It

played over the thin satin gown sweeping down from her shoulders. She lifted her arm, delighted by the feel of the scarlet cloth whispering across her bare skin. It was a completely impractical dress, of course. The desert dust would turn it into a grungy mess in two minutes. It flitted and fluttered everywhere, catching every breeze. No way you could ride a bike in this thing.

And yet…

And yet, it was beautiful. Elegant, with a soft, feminine delicacy she rarely let herself embrace. Standing on the cliff's edge, with the gown whirling about her, she reveled in the strange, new sensations. For one moment, she let her life slip away along with the fears that always hounded her. Of seeming weak. Of being disrespected. Of setting an example for her Pack. For now, nothing existed except her, this gown, and the growing storm.

Until a grouchy voice spoke up behind her. "Wonderful. I have a perfectly lousy day and then I have to dream about *you*."

Lily jumped, startled by that outburst.

Casey Briggs stood glowering at her. Behind him lay a simple stone lean-to, a shelter from the wind's tricks. The entire cabin was filled with an enormous feather bed. Silver lanterns hung from its ceiling and their gleams of light shimmered across the bed's black satin sheets.

She barely noticed. It was *him*, not the bed, she couldn't tear her eyes from.

Even in the desert heat, he favored long shirts that concealed him from her eyes. Stripped of them, clad in nothing but a black loincloth, his body lay revealed before her, a banquet spread before a starving woman.

For some men, strength meant muscles piled on top of muscles until they turned into one beefy column. Not Casey Briggs. He was the perfect wedding of grace and power.

Muscles coiled across his body, yes. And with no softness to hide them, their sharp, taut lines gave quiet witness to his strength. Etched abs, curving biceps, stole her breath away. Yet he moved with elegant ease, muscles flowing, rippling, like water.

They weren't the only surprise his clothes had hidden, either.

Tattoos wove across his body. On his lower arms were the forms she'd glimpsed before. Thick lines, symbols, a sun and moon. They probably had some meaning to his Flight. Maybe they spoke of his oaths and victories in some secret Dragon tongue. To Lily, their meaning was simpler: that was a hell of a lot of blackwork – the most painful kind of tattoo. Those lines might have some ritual or religious meaning to him, but to her, they were a proud boast: Casey Briggs was not a man who shied away from pain.

And his chest…

Over his heart a thunderbird soared, sharp, knife-like wings spread wide. In gentler, curving lines, a horned Dragon circled it. The Native bird caught the eye and held it, painted in broad black stripes across his skin. Yet the Dragon, etched in delicate, breath-taking detail, dazed her. How many hours had he spent under the artist's needle as every scale, every curve of that sinuous body, came to life?

All in black. No bright colors. Just like his clothes and hair.

"I like what my dream did to you," she said with an approving nod. "That ink is a nice addition."

He jumped when she spoke. His eyes, fixed upon the curves of her breasts, jerked up to her face. "And even in my dreams you insist you're in charge."

'His' dream. Again.

Lily shivered. Something was wrong. Dream figures never insisted you were a figment of *their* imaginations. And the details, the sensations… the wind in her hair, the hint of moisture in the wind. They were too rich, too real. She'd never had a dream like this.

Lightning split the sky above. In its wake, she saw an enormous form, a Dragon woven of stars and darkness, stretching across the sky like the Milky Way. Thunder boomed, shockingly close. As its echoes died away, the Dragon spoke in words as loud as the storm.

"NO CLAIM WITHOUT TRUTH!"

No what?

Suddenly, there was something in her hand, something cool, heavy, and smooth.

A cup. A big-ass silver chalice. Which had, apparently, teleported out of nowhere into her hand.

At the same time, a dagger appeared in Casey's fist. Every drop of blood drained from his face as he stared at it. "Oh, Spirits! I know what this is. I know what's happening…"

Well that made *one* of them! Lily tossed the cup onto the bed and rounded on him. "How about you tell me what…"

Pip! The chalice reappeared in her hand.

Indignation lit her face. She cocked her arm and chucked it off the cliff as hard as she could.

"Nooo!" Casey howled. "It's sacred! Don't…!"

Pip! It was back.

"What the hell!" Lily screeched at the cup. Once more, she heaved it away. The Dragon made a half-hearted leap but failed to catch it. Not that it mattered because a second later… *Pip!* No escape!

Cursing and swearing, she fought the stupid thing. Scraping it, throwing it, dropping it and running away. Nothing worked. All the while, Casey yowled something about the 'Rite of Claiming' and sacred rituals and blah blah blah.

If she dropped it and jumped off the cliff herself, would it reappear in mid-air?

Before she could test that theory, a Wolf bounded out of the darkness. As tall as a pony, its ghostly form was spun from mist. Emerald eyes, bright as stars, glowed above its grey muzzle.

Her heart knew it was an ally. "Help me!" she cried, holding out her hand.

With flawless finesse, the Wolf nipped the cup off. Then it leaped from the cliff, running through the air, tail held high.

This time, the cup stayed gone.

Which drove Casey mad with grief. "What the hell have you done?" he wailed. "You've ruined the Rite of Claiming!"

"Yeah, well, you tell your Dragon that the next time it decides to super-glue a cup to my paw, it better ask permission!"

He sank to the ground and buried his face in his hands. A picture of such despair that Lily felt a twinge of remorse.

"Hey." She crouched beside him. "What's going on?"

"This was *supposed* to be the Rite of Claiming."

Some old Dragon ritual. She recalled it, vaguely, from Shifter kids' stories. "That's some rite Dragons do to claim a Mate, right?"

"Yes."

Well, his Dragon was either stoned or stupid – because she had to be the worst potential 'Mate' ever! "Then they make love, right?"

"Yes." He still wouldn't look at her.

"Okay. I think we can work out a compromise here." *Now* she had his attention. "I'm not big into rituals and Claims and whatnot. However, you're hot as hell and I would *love* to jump your bones. So, why don't we skip all the ritual garbage and cut straight to the sex part?"

Her clever offer only made him sigh. "That 'garbage' *is* the

Rite! It transforms a simple union into a pledge of eternal love and devotion!"

Like that was appealing! "Look, my dad taught me that you never buy a car without taking it for a test drive first."

"You can't take love for a 'test drive'!"

"Are you saying you love me?" Her nose wrinkled in disbelieve.

A doubt Casey shared, because he hung his head again. "Not at the moment, no. But... I'm sorry. You don't understand."

"No, I don't – because I'm a Wolf, not a Dragon." Her lips twitched as she fought back a grin. "Do you want to see how Wolves pick a Mate?"

He shrugged, still lost in his own gloom.

That was only going to make this more fun. "First, they make sure the other person is strong. No one wants a weak Mate, after all. Your word is 'bananas.'"

"My what?"

Damn, he had *no* idea what she meant. A heat, fierce and hungry, woke inside her. "Your safe word. If anything happens you don't like, you say that – and it ends."

"I don't under..."

Without warning, Lily pounced on him.

The force of her leap knocked him onto his back. She landed on top and whipped her legs around his hips. As he squirmed, her grip tightened, drawing them close. The heat of his body blazed through the two thin wisps of satin, all that separated them. She felt it burn between her thighs, breathing life onto the desire that smoldered within her. Her body pressed close against his manhood and it stirred under the first lash of passion.

Casey gasped, lips parting under the twin strokes of surprise and lust.

That was her invitation. Her fingers wound through his

hair, pinning him. Then she planted her lips on his. Taking him. Claiming *him*, as a Wolf would do. His mouth, sweet and warm, pressed against hers. Lily slipped her tongue deeper. Tasting, exploring him.

At once, he squirmed, writhing beneath her. Such a feeble 'struggle' didn't free him from the delicious prison of her legs. No, it only served to grind their bodies together. Teasing her most private parts as he rubbed his manhood against the 'bars' that held him.

Her lips released him, and she buried her face in his hair. They found the lobe of his ear and sucked eagerly at it before giving him a playful nip. "I think you're a rabbit," she purred. "A little rabbit who needs to be…"

With a growl, he came to life beneath her. Muscles tightened, bunched… and with one powerful thrust of his hips, he flipped *her* onto her back. "A rabbit, am I?"

Now the tables were turned. *His* weight pressed down upon her, pinning her to the ground. *His* mouth sought hers, claiming her body as his prize.

She twisted, testing the edge of his strength. Muscled arms, powerful thighs, held her; the bars of a prison she didn't truly wish to escape. In their snare, she let herself soften.

As her struggles ebbed, he grew bolder, more confident of her submission. His hand released its grip on her shoulder and began to explore the soft curves of her body, his conquest. It slid down her side, brushing the edge of her breast with a sly, teasing caress. Lower, to cup her buttocks. For one moment, he pulled her up, close against him. Thrusting his ever-growing cock against the folds of her gown – and what she hid beneath it. Then lower still, to slide her leg up over his hips.

Lily's blood sang with joy. With the fierce, passionate union of two Mates. Both strong. Both proud. How easy it would be to surrender to him. To give herself, her body, to his passion.

Not yet. This Wolf was not so easily tamed.

She moaned, arching her back to press herself against his tattooed chest. The slick satin of her gown whispered between them, a thin, frustrating barrier that still kept them apart. Confident that she had succumbed to the call of desire, he rose onto his elbows and sought some way to dispense with the gown's feeble barrier.

That was the opening she needed. Once more, she wrapped her long legs about his hips. This time, though, she bucked, pitching him onto his side. As they spun, she rolled to her feet. One hand lashed out – and caught the knot of his loincloth. A tug, as she scrambled back… and it came free in her hand.

Leaving him, naked, staring up at her in surprise.

"That's the way I like my men!" With a triumphant laugh, she tossed the little shred of cloth into the air. At once, the wind snatched it up and spun it off the cliff.

"Why you…"

With a growl of mock outrage, he bounded to his feet and charged. Lily shrieked with delight and dodged away.

Too slow! His hand caught a billowing fold of her gown. For one second, it held her, bound in his grasp, unable to escape. Then, caught between two forces it could not resist, the satin tore. With the primal, passionate sound of ripping cloth, he tore the dress from her straining body.

Wild longing filled her as he stripped her with that one powerful, irresistible stroke. Now, wind swept across her bare skin. Freed from its cloth prison, her body burned with desire. Damp with yearning, some part of her longed for consummation.

Yet still her Wolfish spirit could not submit. Would not abandon the play of love – quite yet.

As Casey tossed the remnants of her gown away, she dodged around him. Her laughter taunting, begging him to follow her.

But he was fast, her Dragon. Like a striking serpent, he caught her as she leaped past. Arms like steel bands held her, pulled her back… and then lifted her into the air. Tossing her onto his shoulder, as if she weighed no more than the shreds of cloth that flittered off in the wind.

Delighted, she struggled. Kicking. Pounding her fists against his back as he strode toward the shelter and its broad bed. Laughing all the while, with sheer joy at his passion. At the feverish hunger, the haste with which he swept aside all her struggles.

He flung her onto the bed. Its downy expanse caught her, cushioned her. She scrambled to her knees in one last teasing attempt to escape. But Casey swooped down upon her. Catching her. Holding her. Refusing to let this game deny the thirst they both felt, any longer.

Now, she surrendered. To his strength. To her own desire. She had tested her Mate's power – and he did not disappoint.

All that remained was union. To join their bodies in the song, the dance of passion.

Wrapped around her, his hands began to explore her body. Slowly, with unhurried strokes, he took possession of her. They cupped her breasts, gently squeezing, his thumbs circling her aureoles. Every time they whispered across her nipples, she felt herself grow hungrier, more eager. Now, his kisses swept across her shoulders and up along the nape of her neck as he nuzzled aside her short brown curls.

Back arched, eyes closed, Lily gave herself to that pleasure. She could feel the hardness of his cock pressed against the damp eagerness of her sex. Sliding across the slick hairs.

Teasing her, taunting her. Not yet ready to claim the treasure that lay within.

One hand abandoned the pleasure of her breasts and glided lower. Stroking her stomach. Slipping down along her thigh. Then rising back up to the cleft between her legs. With a gasp, she felt his finger slip between the folds of her damp flesh. Seeking, and finding, the nub of her pleasure.

Slowly, surely, he stroked her. Waves of pleasure flooded through her as his finger slipped back and forth. Lily moaned, a harsh, animal cry of need – and felt his cock stiffen, ram-hard, at the sound of her yearning. Shivers swept her body as his caresses grew stronger. Her hips thrusted, grinding against him. Every lash maddened her, made her yearn for him to take her.

Desire burned through her, threatening to overwhelm. With a gasp, she pulled away, fearful that she would lose herself. Sensing no tricks, no rebellion, he let her go. She rolled onto her back and gazed up at him. Hard and masculine, towering above her, his cock jutting proudly into the air. Passion's promise – made flesh.

Panting, their eyes locked. Then she slid her legs wide and welcomed him.

Gently, with perfect control, he lowered himself. Lily felt the length of his long cock slide into her. Filling her, claiming her. She quivered with the sheer joy of holding him inside herself. Claiming him, too, in her own feminine way.

One moment he paused, deep within her.

It was one moment longer than she could bear. With a cry of pure, animal need, Lily dug her fingers into the bedsheets.

That cry, that craving, shattered his proud control. A longing as deep, as endless, as hers swept through him. With a moan, he thrust again and again. Ecstasy swallowed her and her cries; her yearning drove him onward. Faster and faster, each thrust driving them both further into passion's embrace.

Until, with a wail of exquisite joy, she came. Another stroke, another, and a third. Holding that moment, that pinnacle of ecstasy, for one second longer. Then he came, flooding her with his seed.

Panting and exhausted, he collapsed by her side. Lily curled up against him, the sweat of their bodies merging in the desert night.

And for once, she offered no jokes, no play. Fulfilled, satisfied in both heart and soul, she curled against her lover's side until she awoke.

CHAPTER 5

With a rush of adrenaline, Casey awoke – in a new world.

For a moment, he lay still, floating in the river of new emotions that flowed over him. His Dragon, normally so stern and distant, thrummed with delight. Passion left his body languid and fulfilled. Last night, he had fallen asleep, unaware of the hole torn in his soul. This morning, he awoke, healed and whole. Like a blind man who could suddenly see, he understood – for the first time – how beautiful the world could be.

Because of her. That wild, gorgeous, passionate creature.

Who would have guessed that she held such potential under her rough exterior? Casey smiled as he pulled his pants on. She was a diamond in the rough, to be sure. It would take a great deal of work to polish her, to grind off her flaws and make her worthy of the honor his Dragon had bestowed upon her. But he held no doubts, about her *or* her spirit animal. Beneath that leather-clad exterior, that childish rebellion and mad risk-taking, he would find Lily King's true self: a Dragon's Mate.

He rapped gently on the door between their rooms.

"Come in."

Her words, still rough with sleep, set his blood racing. That was his *Mate*, half of his soul, calling to him. He'd intended to speak to her. To discuss their future and what needed to be done. But perhaps the best way to celebrate their union was to repeat the night's ecstasy. The heat that flared in his manhood assured him that yes, he was up to that task. And what better way to honor her than to give her pleasure yet again?

Lily sat by the window, cradling a cup of the motel's cheap instant coffee. Sleep had left her hair deliciously tousled and her t-shirt clung to the curves of her breasts, stirring his desire even further. Yet fatigue lined her delicate face and she did not smile when he entered the room.

All his plans and speeches faded away. Leaving him unsure what to do as the Wolf watched him, guarded and wary.

"How are you?" he managed at last.

"Okay." She shrugged. "Thinking."

No doubt she, too, recognized the enormity of the task ahead of them. In the old days, humans had 'finishing schools', places where young women studied how to behave like proper ladies. Such schools had gone the way of the buffalo. Without them, where did a person even start?

He didn't know... but he wanted to reassure her that they were in this together. Taking the seat near her, he offered his warmest smile. "I imagine this is a lot to process."

"Yeah." She wouldn't meet his gaze, but she seemed calm. "Lot of things to think about."

Such a relief to know that she realized the extent of her problem! "I want you to know that I will help you."

"Help me with what?"

Ice frosted her words, raising red flags in his mind. "Er, changing?"

"Changing *what?*" Her scowl deepened.

Faced with that hostility, Casey felt his arousal drain away. "The things that, uh, need to be changed."

"Like what? Like this coffee?" Lily jabbed a finger at the pale brew. "Are you offering to take me to Starbucks for something that doesn't suck?"

"No. Well, I mean, yes, I'll take you there if you wish." Why were they prattling about coffee on the morning after their Claiming?

"But that's not what you meant by 'things that need changing'?"

"No. I meant...," he hesitated. Surely, she understood? If she didn't, though, he needed to explain. "We're Mates now. That means *you* are a Dragon's Mate. The first in my Flight." The honor of that washed over him and threatened to sweep his speech away in a rush of pride. "That means that certain things will be expected of you."

"Such as?"

A disconcerting quiet lay beneath her words. Was she listening – or preparing to ambush him?

"Well, your dress and behavior, to start. What you do now reflects on my Flight, and thus, you need to present yourself and behave in a way that suits the dignity of the Flight of the Snows."

"There you are with that word again. 'Need'..."

That definitely sounded like a growl... though she hadn't exploded in fury. He took that a positive sign. She may not welcome the changes that lay ahead, but she would understand their urgency. "There's a great deal I'll need to teach you about what angers the spirits. We call it 'Inappropriate Behavior.' No doubt this will require a lot of changes on your behalf, but..."

"Stop. Tell me again why I 'neeeed' to do this?" Lily dragged that word out, transforming it into a sneer.

"You're a Dragon's Mate now. There are expectations."

A howl of laughter burst out of her, harsh and mocking. "Oh, that's rich. Yesterday, your Flight didn't have any Mates at all. Today, you think you've got a Mate *and* 'expectations'!"

Stung, he glared at her. "I don't 'think' anything! We are Mates."

"No, we're not." Lily's lips curled back from canine teeth that had grown long.

Doubt rocked him. They'd shared the Claiming... hadn't they? Something so vivid, so intense, couldn't be a figment of his imagination. "Last night, did you not dream?"

"Yeah, I did. So?"

Thank the spirits! Irritation tempered his relief, though. Why was she being so dense? "That means we're Mates."

Quivering with anger, Lily leaned forward. "Did we run all night beneath the full moon? Did you bring me a rabbit to prove you can feed our pups? Did we howl our love to the moon and receive her blessing? Did we play and wrestle to show our strength?"

Well, okay, maybe they *had* done that bit. Not that Casey seemed to remember. "What's that got to do with anything?" he muttered, puzzled and annoyed.

"*That* is how Wolves pick their Mates."

"Yes, but you don't really have Mates."

The moment those words passed his lips, he longed to call them back. A furious yellow light blossomed in her eyes, turning them into glittering, rage-filled topazes. Every tooth in her mouth sharpened into fangs as she trembled on the edge of Shifting.

Dammit, he had to calm her down! "I'm sorry! That came out wrong. I know that Wolfs form unions like Bears and Hares do."

"And Rats. Rats Mate too."

What a repulsive idea – though this wasn't the time to press that point. "Sure. Of course. But these unions that other Shifters form aren't anything like the Rite of Claiming. A Dragon's Claim is sacred."

"So are Wolves' rituals!"

"Look…" He, too, leaned forward, braving her wrath. Hoping that his openness would calm her down. "You know I'm right. You were there last night, at the Rite of Claiming."

"We shared a dream. Big deal! Okay, so the sex was hot. But it didn't mean anything."

"It *means* that my Dragon chose you to be my Mate!"

Lily folded her arms across her chest. "Sucks to be you, then, because my Wolf sure as hell didn't Claim you."

"But…"

"But nothing. We're not Mates. I don't 'Claim' you, jerk. And hey!" A vindictive glee brightened her face. "Isn't the Rite of Claiming supposed to have a 'rite' in it? Because I seem to remember that my Wolf ran off with that stupid goblet before anybody got Claimed."

Oh damn, she had a point. The color drained from his face as he considered it. According to the legends, yes, the Rite of Claiming had several stages. Last night started smoothly, with the Invocation of Truth. But… yeah. Several things were supposed to come after that, like the Symbolic Marriage where cup and dagger were united. He and Lily had kind of skipped all that and jumped straight to the sex…

"Ha!" she crowed. "That's what I thought! We're not Mates, not by your rules *or* mine!"

"But… but we…"

She rose to her feet, glowering down at him. "So, since we're *not* Mates, why don't you get out of my room and let me get dressed. We've got a long ride back to Ringo's Spread."

"No, we need to go to the Sierra Nevadas. My Alpha will know what to do."

"You can go to California if you want. I'm going home."

"No, I'm still your bodyguard. Now more than ever, it's critical that I stay with you."

"Then I guess you're going to the Spread," she purred with pure malice, "'cuz I am. Now *get out!*"

BACK IN HIS ROOM, HEAD SPINNING, CASEY CALLED HOME. Maybe a trip to the Lair was out of the question, but he needed his Alpha's advice.

Badly.

"Miles Kennedy." His Alpha's baritone was a balm on his rattled nerves. Reserved, dignified, and confident, it promised answers to his questions.

"Greetings to you, Wisest of the Flight."

"Greetings to you, Son of the Wind."

That ritual greeting, so familiar, was another sweet breeze of comfort. "I need advice. Strange and terrible things have happened."

Quickly, he laid out the events of the last twenty-four hours. How Aaron King had requested repayment of his Blood Debt. Lily's reaction. And then, halting and ashamed, he described the dream they'd shared and the botched mess he'd made of the Rite of Claiming.

When he finished, Kennedy said nothing. The silence stretched on, making Casey squirm. "I need your counsel, Alpha," he urged at last. "What should I do?"

"Your greatest duty is, and remains, fulfilling the Blood Debt." Solid words, spoken with gravity and confidence. Or were they? Was there a waver, a hint of doubt, that colored them?

"Is the Duty of Blood truly greater than the Rite of Claiming?"

"Yes." *That* was sure. Whatever doubt he'd thought he'd heard was gone now. "The Duty of Blood is the greatest honor a Dragon can know."

"Greater than Claiming and the Duty to Mate? Greater than the Protection of Wellsprings?"

"Yes, because the Duty of Blood exists. Wellsprings and Claiming are just fairy tales, no matter what those fools in the 'First' Flight claim."

Two weeks ago, he would have agreed. But at Rex Fairburn's meeting, a half-dozen Hares supported the First Flight's crazy stories of living Wellsprings. And nothing, not even a direct pronouncement from his Alpha, could make him doubt the truth of what he and Lily shared last night.

So, he did the unthinkable: he challenged his leader. "Respectfully, you are wrong. Many Shifters have seen these Wellsprings. And the Rite is… unmistakable."

"There is nothing 'respectful' about defiance," Kennedy snarled.

In person, an Alpha had many tricks to cow an insubordinate Dragon. His tone, his burning gaze, the strength of his posture… all served to weaken the will of those who defied him.

Phones, however, defeated most of those stratagems and Casey stuck to his guns. "There is no defiance in correcting misinformation. You didn't hear the Hares' testimony, nor did you experience the dream that Lily King and I shared. I cannot doubt that the Wellsprings have returned – and they've brought the Rite of Claiming back with them."

"That remains to be seen," Kennedy snapped. "Yet, even if they have, it changes nothing. You owe a duty to Aaron King. You have sworn, as a defender of our Flight, to protect his daughter. Debauching her shatters that oath. It is Incorrect Behavior. It shames our Flight."

Each accusation hit him like the blow of a sledgehammer. "I did not defile her! The Rite of Claiming is sacred!"

"By your own admission, she does not consider herself Claimed."

"Well, she's wrong!" he snapped.

Confident and in charge once again, Kennedy grew stern. "The Rite of Claiming can *never* be done without consent. You know that. Every story, every legend, makes this plain. If she says she is not Claimed, she is not."

Casey's thoughts whirled in chaos. "But the dream... it was so real... my Dragon..."

"...did not Claim her. There was no Rite of Claiming. Just a strange dream that offered serious insult to the oath you swore."

"It was..."

"It was sex. Nothing more. Not sacred. Not Claiming. Nothing."

His Dragon railed against that. It knew, even if his Alpha did not, that the two of them belonged together. That Fate or Destiny linked them, for all times.

Yet Casey, the man, could not agree with it. His Alpha was right. Without consent, without ritual, no Claim existed. "What should I do then?" he whispered.

"Your duty." In charge once more, Kennedy didn't hesitate. "Protect this woman, as you swore you would. Repay the Blood Debt our Flight owes. Do not touch her or look upon her with lust. *That* is Correct Behavior."

Maybe. But it sounded plain old 'impossible' to him!

CHAPTER 6

The only thing worse than getting baby-sat was getting baby-sat by a smoking-hot sitter you couldn't touch.

Under the scorching sun, June burned its way into July. Three miserable weeks passed at Ringo's Spread. No matter where Lily went, she was never alone. He was always there. Casey Briggs. Flying overhead. Trailing her bike, three car-lengths back. Lurking at the edge of the crowd in the evenings, when her Pack drank and danced by the fire. Keeping her 'safe'.

Damn, that word made her sick!

Life would be so much easier if she could just hate his smug, arrogant, aristocratic face. But the dream complicated everything.

It returned to her in flashes, when she least expected it. She'd catch a glimpse of him skulking outside her trailer in the evening. 'Checking for threats.' And instead of laughing at his paranoia, as she ought to, she was swept away by memories. The power of his arms as he tossed her onto the bed, the flash of excitement she felt as he pinned her there, taking her as she longed to be taken.

Ten seconds later she'd come to her senses, all sarcastic jokes forgotten. Realizing, to her shame, that she stared at him with open longing, passion singing through her blood. Wishing, *yearning* for him to come back and take her, here and now.

Which he never did. If he noticed her desire, he gave no sign. He never looked at her like a man did, not after that first enraging morning when he stormed into her room with his stupid ideas about 'changing' her. For all the rough play of their love-making, Casey Briggs was a man who understood what the word 'no' meant.

That ought to make her happy. But as she watched him, tucked into a bit of shade and scanning the horizon with binoculars, frustration – not pleasure – filled her.

Okay, so the guy understands 'no.' How about 'maybe'? Or, 'Eh, I'm not really into this whole Eternal Commitment thing, but I'll happily jump your bones.'

Yeah, no. Casey Briggs wasn't a man who understood hook-ups, one-night stands, or friends with benefits. It was all or nothing with him. Now, she could respect that. Wolves Mated for life and she fully expected to settle down with someone. But not a Dragon. Not Casey. The dude came with a whole lot of baggage; he'd made that clear on the first morning. Baggage he expected *her* to carry.

And Lily King was not lugging any man's crap around. She didn't 'clean up' well. She wasn't going to change to please some stuck-up Dragon no matter how loudly he screamed that they were 'destined' to be together.

Screw Fate. Screw him. She was her own boss.

She took a sip of her beer, relaxing as the icy liquid poured down her throat. Breakfast of Champions!

Beside her, Ghost snickered.

Immediately, Lily spun to stare at her. No Alpha needed a babysitter, or a bodyguard, or whatever the hell Casey wanted to call himself. So of course, when her father 'assigned' her one, the whole Pack took it as a vote of no confidence. And, as Wolves did, they started testing her. Taking her last beer. Bumping her bike over when they parked. Interrupting her when she spoke. A dozen tiny challenges each day, probing to see if she really had grown weak.

Every act of defiance she slapped down, fast. They didn't anger her, though. Wolves tested their leaders. That was their nature. That was the Way. When your Pack nipped at you, you didn't take it personally. But you *did* snap back.

Even when the person nipping was your best friend. "What's so funny?"

"You." Impish delight lit Ghost's face and behind them her Wolf hopped about playfully, as if daring Lily to chase it. "You can't take your eyes off that Dragon, can you?"

"He just annoys the hell out of me," she protested. "Ignore pests and you end up with fleas."

"Butt fleas?"

Lily tried to lock eyes with the other woman, but Ghost kept watching Casey. "What are you going on about?"

"Butt fleas. I figure that must be what you're worried about, because you keep staring at his ass."

"I am *not* staring at his… at his…"

And, of course, the accusation alone made her glance back at the Dragon. Where… yes, she found herself ogling the sleek, taut muscles of his…

"Dammit."

Oh, Ghost's Wolf was prancing now! "Those fleas must be running from his toes to his head now because you're…"

"Shaddup!" Shaking her head, Lily rose and grabbed herself another beer.

"Hey, where's mine!" Ghost complained.

"Get your own!" Alphas did *not* wait on other people!

But, of course, Ghost had a cooler beside her wheelchair. Laughing, she retrieved another bottle from it. "Admit it: he's hot as hell. Why are you so hung up about that?"

"I don't like him."

"Since when has that ever stopped you from sleeping with a guy?"

Oh, nipped – and nipped hard! Lily's own Wolf bristled with outrage. "It's complicated."

"Why? If he's gonna be underfoot all the time, you might as well have some fun. Or is sex a no-no for bodyguards? Too distracting?"

"Probably, yeah, but…"

Oh, what the hell. Time to come clean. Embarrassing as it was, she longed to confide in her friend. "He thinks we're Mates."

Ghost choked on her beer – a satisfying sound. "What?!? Why?"

"We shared this weird dream and, like, had sex in it. Or something."

An undignified squeak of excitement escaped her friend. "Was it the Rite of Claiming?"

"Yes? No? Maybe?" Lilly tossed her arms wide, spilling a bit of beer onto the ground. "How should I know? There wasn't any 'rite' but, well, some ghostly Dragon did yell something about 'claiming.'"

"Oh wow!" Ghost breathed, staring at her like she was Cinderella or some other Disney princess.

Before she got too enthused, Lily dropped the bomb shell. "Then the next morning he stomps into my room with a long list of all the ways I need to change if I want to be 'worthy' of being a Dragon's Mate."

As she'd hoped, her friend's jaw dropped. "Screw that!" she snapped.

"Exactly." Lily saluted her with her beer. Meanwhile her pleased Wolf settled to the ground, feeling like all its fur had been licked into place.

Both of them glared across the hot sand at Casey. In the midst of a phone call, the Dragon didn't notice their indignation.

Ghost was the first to look away, worry wrinkling her brow. "What happens when someone doesn't agree to be 'Claimed'? Are you actually Mates or not?"

"I have no idea."

"Are you going to ask?"

"Who? Him?" Lily snorted. "He'll say 'yes', of course."

"What about some other Dragon?"

"You think anyone in his Flight will be less stuck up? Nah."

"Wasn't there a Dragon from the First Flight at that meeting you went to?"

"Rex Fairburn's thing? Yeah. Finn... Donaldson. Or something like that." Lily struggled to recall anything about him. "We didn't talk. Big brute – wouldn't want to get in a fight with him. And damn did he love cocktail wieners! I think he tossed back five pounds of the things."

Ghost chuckled. "Well that sounds hopeful. I mean, most Dragons would starve before they debased themselves by eating a hot dog."

Maybe. But that didn't make the subject any less humiliating. Lily shook her head. "I don't need to talk to him because I already know the answer: no dream 'makes' me anything I don't want to be."

"But don't you want to find out..."

"No." She added a bit of force to the word to kill that line of questioning.

"Okay. You're the Alpha."

Said with all innocence and oh so very sweetly! Lily glowered at her friend, sure she was up to something.

Before she could drag the answer out of her, though, a sudden movement drew her attention. Out beyond the Spread's circle of trailers, the air shimmered as a horned black Dragon flew in tight loops, snapping its jaws at nothing.

"Whoa," Ghost murmured. "What's wrong with your bodyguard?"

"Don't know." Casey himself stood still, his hands jammed in his pockets, staring off into the distance. Only his Dragon betrayed the emotions that tore him apart. "Guess he got bad news on that phone call."

Best to check. That Dragon would spook every Wolf in the Pack if it kept up those acrobatics.

As she strolled over, Casey hissed something to his Dragon. The great serpent settled to the ground, but its tail continued to whip back and forth furiously.

"Lily."

At least they'd gotten past the ridiculous 'Ms. King.' "What's up?"

"Nothing that concerns you." Swish, swish, swish went the Dragon's tail.

"Wrong." She pointed at his irate spirit. "You think our Wolves can't see that? It's like having someone pet your fur backwards. By lunch every person in the Spread is going to be at each other's throat. So, spit it out. What happened?"

Teeth gritted, he glared at his Dragon. It stared back, lips curled to reveal a maw full of six-inch fangs. Made Lily glad her own spirit animal was a lot less intimidating. "My Alpha called. A thief broke into our Lair."

She couldn't help it: her jaw dropped, and she gaped about Casey like a startled puppy. "Someone broke into the

Lair of a Flight of Dragons?!? Holy crap! The *balls* on that guy!"

Her shocked admiration annoyed him. "More like 'brains' – or lack of brains! The man must be a complete moron to anger us."

"So, what'd this 'moron' take? Your tv? The penny jar in your kitchen?"

"No, of course not!" Dragons didn't like being nipped. Which made the game all the more fun. "He penetrated the Sanctum, where we keep the Flight's most precious belongings."

"Okay that doesn't sound like a 'moron' to me. That's a guy with brass balls. How much was the stuff worth? Maybe we can find him that way. There aren't too many fences who'll handle big-ticket items."

"That's the strangest part." His Dragon took to the air again and resumed its restless spinning. "He stole almost nothing. The Sanctum is full of priceless artifacts, yet he walked past all of them and took only one thing: a clay pot."

"Magic?"

"No. The pot itself was nothing special. It held some cornmeal, turquoise dust, and a small carving of an eagle."

"Like a Zuni fetish?" she asked. The Dragon nodded. "Was *that* magical?"

"No, though it was sacred. A token of respect, given to my Flight by the spirit of a holy mountain."

"But it didn't do anything?"

"It showed respect." Both man and Dragon growled.

"Calm down. I'm just trying to figure out why a thief would want it." The warning from Rex Fairburn's meeting echoed in her mind. "You remember what the First Flight said? With the return of the Wellsprings, old artifacts are developing magic powers. Or, well, regaining their old strength."

"If you believe the 'First' Flight," he sniffed.

"I do. Because my necklace used to Shift with me."

Not much he could say against that. Casey shrugged. "Point taken. Though this fetish has done nothing unusual."

And that brought them right back to square one. "What about the cornmeal and ground turquoise?"

"Bought from a store."

"Why?"

"To honor the fetish."

Honoring… rocks. Wow, the Flight of the Snows was a bunch of weirdos. "So, a guy sneaks into the home of the most dangerous, lethal creatures on this planet. He ignores all their riches and only takes a worthless pot full of junk and a rock that doesn't do anything. Does the pot at least look cool?"

"No. It's plain and in a cabinet out of sight. We wouldn't even know that it was gone – except that Dragons know their Lair. We can sense when something is missing."

At that, her Wolf bounded to attention, ears pricked up. "But you guys didn't feel it being taken? You know what that means, right? Your thief not only had balls and a plan, he had magic to hide from you. This isn't some random meth-head trying to get his next score. This is bad."

In fact, it sounded like those damned Fangs of Apophis again.

"I know." Casey hung his head, dejected.

Geez, it didn't take much to knock the wind out of him! Lily rolled her eyes. "So, you willing to 'live on the edge' and borrow someone's bike? Or are we driving all the way to California in that stupid car of yours?"

His Dragon's endless whirling finally ceased. It plunked to the ground, lowered its head, and sniffed gently at her. "Why would we go to California?"

"That's where your Lair is, right? We're not going to figure out what happened if we stay here in Colorado."

"My Flight will handle this."

"You don't want to help?"

His teeth ground together, hard enough for her to hear. "My duty is here. With you."

"So, if I go to California, your duty will be in California. Where you can help figure out what happened." Lily grinned at him.

A smile he did not return. "No. It could be dangerous. My duty to you comes first."

That was a creepy sentiment. Her Wolf's fur bristled. "For us, the Pack comes first."

His chin rose, though a shadow darkened his face. "I'm a Dragon, not a Wolf. Honor and duty reign supreme in our Lairs. You cannot abandon them, even if the Flight suffers."

And no matter how much it hurt *him*. Lily felt a grudging respect. Her bodyguard might be a pompous idiot – but his spirit was true and strong. He'd stay here and guard her, no matter how much it cost him.

If she let him.

"Yeah well that's why Wolves don't volunteer for 'duties' and 'honors'. That way you don't have to choose between them and your Pack. So, I guess it's the bike, then."

"The bike?" His frown set her Wolf prancing with delight. He didn't even see the trap right in front of his feet. "What bike?"

"The bike I'm riding to California."

"We're not going to my Flight. I already told you that!"

"*I'm* going." She glanced at him over her shoulder as she turned away, eyes sparkling. "You coming too? Or is my babysitter gonna let me do this solo?"

As she expected, he tagged along.

CHAPTER 7

In the end, they didn't take either the motorcycle or the car. One of her Pack dropped them off at Johnson's Airport – a strip of packed dirt that really didn't deserve its name. A quick call to the Flight summoned a sparkling clean Piper Cherokee 4-seater that whisked them over to the Sierra Nevada Mountains.

Her first glimpse of the Aerie (as Casey referred to his home) left Lily speechless. High in the Sierras, surrounded by snow-capped mountains even in the middle of summer, the Aerie sprawled along a ridge. Three stories of broad windows offered breath-taking views down the valley. Statues and fountains graced the small lawn that lay before it, allowing its guests to drink in that luscious view as they took their strolls.

"How many Dragons are in your Flight?" Lily asked. Hell, most resorts weren't this large!

"Eight," Casey replied.

"All of this for *eight* people?"

Her disbelief seemed to offend him slightly. "Plus, servants."

'Servants.' Of course, they had 'servants.' "Damn, you guys must be seriously incompetent if you need that many people to take care of you!"

Ignoring his scowl, she peered out the plane's window, surveying the land. Five miles of winding private road lay between the Aerie and civilization.

"Gated?"

"Yes. With a guard post."

No way they'd let some lost tourist wander up into their little preserve! Though it did leave her wondering how the thief made his escape. In the dark, over mountainous terrain, five miles was a long hike.

At the end of the ridge lay a neat, paved private airstrip for gimp guests like her who couldn't just Shift into a Dragon and fly in by themselves. A 'servant' awaited them. He made a serious attempt to take Lily's backpack before she chased him off. Let him carry the Dragon's junk. Wolves didn't need – or want – to be fawned upon. Eventually he gave up and led them through the Aerie's empty, echoing marble hallways to her 'rooms'. A 'little suite' that was as large as her place back at the Spread. And a helluva lot cleaner.

It even had its own private 'servants' quarters', a small room attached to the suite's living room. Casey stashed his gear there.

"You don't even rate a room?"

"I am your bodyguard," he reminded her, with wounded pride. "It would be inappropriate for me to lodge far away."

"You think I'm going to get attacked in the middle of a Lair?"

"No. Though I didn't expect a thief, either."

Eh, good point.

"Besides," he continued, "with your manners you may well provoke one of my Brethren into an assault."

Was that… a joke? Hard to tell; Casey didn't crack a smile,

but her Wolf's tail rose anyway. "Glad to know you've got my back if that happens!"

Another servant appeared. She could tell he wasn't a Dragon because all the staff wore these tidy black suits with white gloves. *And* they spoke like extras from a horror movie. "Master Briggs, Lord Kennedy bids me offer welcome to you and our lady guest."

Master. Lord…

Bile rose in Lily's throat. With it came a wild desire to Shift and flee through the halls, biting anyone who got in her way. This place was a crypt. Beautiful yet suffocating, burying everyone under the weight of its dust and age.

Run! her Wolf urged. *Escape!*

And the worst part? Casey still thought she was 'meant' to be his Mate. He expected her to join him here, in this mausoleum.

The thought horrified her. It sent shivers down her spine, worse than a hundred fleas.

Run! Run, run, run, flee!

No. Lily forced her mind away from thoughts of the woods, cool, green, and rich with the scent of pine. Sure, this place was a trap. But she was smart. She could walk through it, do her job, and escape.

Casey studied her, his expression clouded. "Are you alright?"

"Yeah. Fine." Guess she hadn't hidden her revulsion as well as she thought.

The servant bowed to her. "Does my lady require anything?"

I don't know. Why don't you go ask her?

Lily bit her lip before the words escaped and shook her head. Her Wolf simply shuddered.

"Then Lord Kennedy requests the honor of your presence

in the Green Room, once you have had an opportunity to freshen up."

"This is as fresh as I get, buddy!"

A whine escaped her poor Wolf. *Woods! Free! Run!*

Casey stepped in before a real spat could arise. "Thank you. Please convey our gratitude for His Lordship's hospitality. We will attend upon him momentarily."

Bowing, the servant backed out of the suite. *Backed!* Like they were royalty and he didn't dare turn away from them.

Shivers swept over Lily as Wolf-mind crept close. She gritted her teeth, breathed hard... and kept herself together.

Until that door closed.

The moment the servant's footsteps faded away, she set her Wolf loose.

Her legs gave way and she fell, fur and fangs springing forth. Dull-clawed paws hit the ground running, scrabbling for traction on the slick stone floor. And then she was bolting, fleeing, flying towards the balcony doors.

"Lily!" her bodyguard roared.

No escape! The doors were closed! She leaped into the air, twisting and kicking off from the thick glass that trapped her. Casey dove for her, but the two-legged fool was slow, slow, slow! She dodged his arms, jumped onto the couch and sprang away.

Skittering into the bathroom... no escape there! As he blundered into the doorway, she ricocheted off the claw-footed tub and darted past him down the hall. One hand snatched at her fur, caught her tail for a second before she slipped free, howling with glee.

Free! Free at last to escape into the...

No! This was a bedroom! Another snare of walls and glass! No way out except the door – where *he* stood now, yelling nonsense and waving his arms. She was trapped! Trapped!

Something needed to die.

Lily chose the pillow.

She leaped on the bed and sank her fangs deep into one of its huge pillows. Teeth tore through Egyptian cotton. Then she whipped her head back and forth, side to side, savaging it.

Cloth tore. Feathers exploded out, filling the air with snowy down. Snarling she whirled, her short claws ripping holes in the bed spread. And still she worried the pillow, shaking it, tearing it, spilling its feathery guts everywhere.

When the pillow was thoroughly dead, she dropped its gutted husk and tottered off the bed. Lights flickered and her sleek, Wolfen form Shifted back to human. Exhausted but calm, Lily flopped on the floor and panted.

In the doorway, Casey stared at her slack jawed. "What. The. Hell?"

"Sorry!" she gasped. "Little bit of… claustrophobia!"

"Are you mad?" He inched forward, circling around her as if she was rabid.

"Nope! I'm good."

"You're 'good'?" Feathers drifted down past his face.

"Yup." Still breathing hard, she managed to sit up. "Thought I'd get that out of my system *before* I went to talk to your Alpha."

He stared. At her, gasping on the floor. At dusting of feathers that now covered the room. At the bedspread, torn and rumbled. Then he coughed. "On further consideration, I withdraw my objection. That *was* a good idea."

"Knew you'd see it my way." She held out a hand. Casey took it and pulled her to her feet. "So, shall we go see your Alpha?"

. . .

Miles Kennedy was every bit as bad as she'd feared. Tall and regal, with the prominent nose of a Roman emperor, he relaxed in his two-story library. Thick curtains of green velvet hung between shelves – the source of the name 'Green Room', Lily guessed. Kennedy rose from behind a gleaming mahogany desk. Black suit, gold cufflinks... even a neatly folded handkerchief peeking out of his breast pocket. From his perfectly coiffed brown hair to the manicured nails on the hand he offered, no flaw or speck of dust dared to show its face.

"Daughter of our ally, know that you are welcome here, in the Aerie.

Good thing her Wolf was exhausted from all that pillow-slaughter! A greeting like that would send it howling for the hills. What the hell was wrong with just saying, 'Hey!' or 'How's it going?'

Come to think of it, what was she supposed to say now? "Uh... thanks?" was all she could manage quickly. Though she did shake his hand with a firm grip.

"The strength of the Flight of the Snows surrounds you and shields you."

Uh-huh. A 'strength' that a thief had just popped like a water balloon.

"We honor the debt of blood that unites us. Tell me: how may my Flight assist you?"

Beside her, Casey winced as formalities piled on top of each other. That grimace was like a breath of fresh air. Did he see, now, how stilted and hidebound his Flight had become? Had three weeks with her Pack taught him to be normal?

If a Pack of crazy Wolves were 'normal', that is. Yeah, on second thought, that was probably too much to hope for. But at least her bodyguard was starting to 'unbutton' a bit.

"Actually, I'm hoping I can help *you*. Casey tells me that you had a break-in. I can help you find the thief."

Kennedy blinked. His lips pinched together in a little 'O' of surprise, like someone had crept up behind him and pinched him on the butt. Her spirits rose at the sight – and even her exhausted Wolf raised its head.

Play?

Nah, not right now. Work first, play later.

The Wolf's head flopped back down. *Too tired. No work.*

The Alpha recovered from his surprise quickly and, as she'd expected, brushed away her offer. "Your consideration is a testament to your character. Know, however, that my Flight possesses ample power to defend itself and the treasures of its Lair."

"Really? Because I heard you lost a pot and the thief got away clean."

Kennedy turned a baleful stare on Casey.

Oopsies. She might be getting her sitter in hot water. Annoying as he was, she didn't want that. Time to draw the Alpha's attention back to her. "Hey, Mr. Kennedy. Nice nose you've got."

"Excuse me?" As she'd hoped, in his confusion he completely forgot her bodyguard.

"Big. Strong. A nose to be reckoned with." Lily nodded, delighted by his bafflement. "How well can it smell, though?"

"I don't follow you."

"My nose works *great*. It may be smaller than yours, but it can tell me where every person in this house has gone in the last three days. Show me where your pot was, and I'll take you to where your thief is."

Like two statues, the men studied her. Kennedy's Dragon reared slowly, offended. Lips curved away from teeth as it loomed above her. That silent threat sent a jolt of alarm through her Wolf. But as her spirit animal scrambled to its feet, a shadow rose above it.

No, not a shadow. A sinuous, elegant black Dragon rose behind her Wolf, spreading its wings wide to shield her.

Casey's Dragon. Defying his Alpha. Protecting *her*.

Eyes locked, the two great serpents glared at each, filling the room with silent menace. Neither was willing to back down.

But Kennedy was in the wrong – and he knew it. Nobody, not even Wolves, thought that bullying your guests was good manners. And so, he was the first to glance away.

"Again, your generosity honors you. However, we do not need assistance."

"Can you track your thief? I can."

"The thief will be located. This matter does not concern you."

"If you just show me where the pot was, I can…"

"That is impossible." Annoyance sharpened his words. Like most Alphas, Kennedy didn't handle 'rebellion' well. "None but my Flight ever enters the Sanctum."

Must get pretty dusty in there. She couldn't picture Dragons cleaning up. "Okay, but I can…"

"No." Cold and implacable, that one word killed all debate. "*No one* enters."

Fine. She could work around their idiot rules. "Then show me the door to the Sanctum. I assume there's only one, right? A choke-point? Security? Your Sanctum doesn't have six different entrances that let any idiot wander in, right?"

Kennedy's Dragon seethed, even though the Alpha kept his face cool and impassive. "This serves no useful purpose."

Once more Casey came to her rescue. "Yet it is a small request, easily granted. Surely the debt between us weighs upon this matter? If we can so easily oblige, does honor not demand we acquiesce?"

That must be snob-speak for 'please.' Lily held herself still – well, as still as an agitated Wolf could manage – while the Alpha pondered.

"Very well. We will grant you this honor."

The… 'honor' of looking at a door?

Bite. Run. Howl. Flee, her Wolf urged.

Not yet. Later, though…

"Thanks." She even managed to smile… kind of. Probably not very convincing.

Fortunately, Kennedy abandoned his speeches. In silence he led them through the Aerie's tall, echoing halls. Past endless paintings of the stern Dragons of yester-years. Down one flight of stairs and then another. No elevators for these guys. Nope, nope, nope. As they threaded through the maze of marble floors and dark wood paneling, Lily found herself wondering again how a thief had even managed to find this 'Sanctum.'

A corridor in the sub-basement ended at a thick iron door.

Lily gazed around her. No surveillance cameras. No security system that she could see. Nothing except a big locked door to defend all their treasures.

Okay, a big locked door AND a Flight of Dragons that can tell the moment you touch their stuff. I can see why they're not too worried.

"The Sanctum," Kennedy intoned.

"Cool." Lily Shifted and snuffled, drawing in deep mouthfuls of the chill, musty air. Like every Shifter, the Alpha stared at her necklace. The Thing That Wouldn't Shift. A piece of magic as subtle as a blinking neon light.

Screw it. Let him stare all he wanted. She had work to do.

Up and down the hall she ranged, nose to the ground. By the time she circled back to sniff the door knob, she knew exactly what had happened.

"Right!" Leaping onto her hind legs, she Shifted back. "Got it. Let's go find her."

"'Her' who?" Casey said.

"Your thief. Turns out she doesn't have an enormous pair of balls – she's got breasts. I should have guessed she was a woman because, honestly, breasts are a *lot* bigger than balls."

Neither Dragon laughed at her joke. Through pinched lips, Kennedy hissed, "I would ask you to offer me the courtesy of an explanation."

"Sure thing!" She waved at the hall around them. "Not a lot of traffic down here, so the layout is pretty clear. I smell three things. Bunch of Dragons – check, they belong. The guy who brought us your message. Is he authorized to be down here?"

"Morrison? Yes. Alone of the servants, he tends this floor."

Lucky him. Lily managed *not* to roll her eyes. "So, none of your female servants come down here?"

Affronted, Kennedy straightened. "There are no women at the Aerie. It would be inappropriate."

"No girls at the Dragon Monastery. Check." Beside her, Casey twitched. Lily ignored him and plowed on. "Then the woman who came here has to be our thief. She walked down the hall, picked this lock. Went it, came out. Left."

"Mortal or Shifter?" Casey asked.

"That's the big question. I *ought* to be able to tell – and I can't. There's a hint of something rank, like a Rat. But it's not clear. I bet that's part of whatever magical protections your thief had."

Kennedy frowned, clearly not pleased to have the conversation spiral out of his control. "We have no evidence that this burglar possessed magical skills or protection."

"Sure, we do. You didn't notice when she stole your crap. I assume that requires magic, right? Or do Dragons sometimes get so caught up in cat videos on YouTube that they don't notice people robbing their Lairs?"

Casey shot her a despairing look as his Alpha snarled, "We do *not!*"

"Good. So, magic it is."

Kennedy gritted his teeth. "I thank you for this information." Every word was spat out, like the courtesy pained him. "We will take it into consideration."

"Consider away. Meanwhile, I'm gonna go find your thief."

"Miss King..." The Dragon raised a hand as she backed away.

"No need to see me out. I can track myself, too." Cheered by the prospect of escaping this gilded tomb, her Wolf bounded down the hall. "You coming, bodyguard?"

Without pausing for his answer, she spun and followed her Wolf.

CHAPTER 8

They made it all the way to the driveway before Casey's frustration boiled over. "You couldn't resist, could you?"

Lily paused. "Resist what?"

"Mocking my Alpha!"

Even this simple fact seemed to confuse her. "I thought I was pretty damned polite, all things considered."

"Cat videos? Dragon Monastery?" he fumed. "Not to mention the mess you left in our rooms."

"Casey, I'm a Wolf. We're not house-broken. Hell, even dogs chew slippers. Wolves are way worse."

This. *This* was the woman Fate chose for him?

Shaking his head, he glared up at the sun. How could the spirits mock him so viciously? There had *never* been a woman so unsuitable for the honor of being a Dragon's Mate!

His thoughts must have been written across his face, because when his gaze dropped, he found Lily watching him, lips twisted into a hard, humorless grin. "Now aren't you glad we decided to dump all this 'Mate' BS?"

"Yes, I am!" In truth, that was *her* decision, not his. *He* was willing to accept his fate. *He* had offered to help her fit into a Dragon's world. But now?

Now he rejoiced. Lily King was rude, uncouth, and unsophisticated. He would *never* consent to be her Mate!

His Dragon keened, sickened by his anger. Lily and her Wolf simply turned away. "Good. Glad there's one thing we agree on. Now let's go find your thief."

Shifting, she trotted along the drive until she found the robber's scent. Casey took to the air, wrapping himself in Brother Wind's cloak so that no mortal would see him. Lily slipped into the dark forest and loped away, seeking her prey. Circling above her, it took all his attention to follow her as she padded off, hidden by dense branches.

Attention came hard, too, because his mind kept wandering back to the Aerie. And her. Her flippant jokes. Her brash refusal to make herself presentable. The madness that a simple invitation evoked in her. Who the hell destroyed their room like that?

One sour note ruined his song of outrage.

Respect.

Soft at first, it swelled as the Wolf cut through the woods. She was good, the best tracker he'd ever seen. Two minutes in that hall was all she needed to figure out exactly what had happened. Now she arrowed through the Sierras at a full run, hot on the trail of their enemy.

His enemy, not hers. Yet she hunted the foe as eagerly as if she herself had been wronged.

He... respected that.

Resented it too, of course! He shook his head, trying to summon back the warm mantle of indignation. She was his ward, the woman he was bound to protect. Why couldn't she accept that? Why did she throw herself into danger? Why did she take risks that could destroy his honor completely?

She is our Mate? his Dragon suggested. Almost hesitantly.

But she wasn't! She'd made a shamble of the Rite of Claiming.

Rebuffed, his Dragon fell silent and scanned for glimpses of Lily's brown fur.

When they reached the valley road, the Wolf Shifted back and waved him down.

"Think we're dealing with more than one person." With no thought for her dignity, she flopped onto the ground, panting. "Somebody dropped our thief off. She climbed this ridge slowly, carrying a mountain bike. After the heist she rode it down. Fast." A grin of pure Wolfish admiration spread across her face. "Nearly wiped out a couple of times. I'm kinda surprised we didn't find her wrapped around a tree halfway down."

"And then?"

"The same car picked her up. Give me a sec to catch my breath and we'll see where they went."

"You can track cars? On roads?" That annoying respect grew stronger.

"Yeah. Gift of my necklace. Though if they hop on a free-way, we're screwed. I can't run that fast."

Fortune favored them – at first.

The trail led to the Desert Inn, a run-down strip motel just off the highway. Brazen as a coyote, Lily trotted through the parking lot and up to the door of Room 113.

Casey himself Shifted back and hurried after her. "What if someone sees you?" he muttered as she sniffed the door.

Lights danced around her, sparkling across the empty lot. "Then I'll bark and wag my tail and every damned fool will think I'm somebody's pet wolf-dog," she chuckled, as she stood up.

She did have a point. Wolves didn't derange mortals the way Dragons did.

"Bad news. The room smells of laundry detergent and cleaner. Our thieves – a man and a woman – are gone. Hours gone, by the smell of it." She glanced across the scrub at the cars whizzing past on the highway. "And I'm guessing they hopped on that."

"So, the trail ends here." Disappointing, but not surprising.

"No, the trail gets challenging here." Alive with the joy of the hunt, she nearly bounced from foot to foot.

This… excited her? His temper flared for one moment. An assault on his Lair was a grievous affront. How dare she treat it like a game?

Because all of life is a game to her.

Love, battle, hunting… it didn't matter what she did. Lily savored every second of her life. She lived in the moment, throwing herself at every pleasure, every danger with complete abandon.

He knew that, but he couldn't quite wrap his head around it. His own life moved slowly, each act surrounded by thought and consideration. Was this deed appropriate? Would it offend the spirits or bring reproach to his Flight?

What would it be like to throw caution to the wind? To be like her. To want and act in the same moment and let the future care for itself.

There was a seduction, an allure to that – but he rejected it. Wisdom, not pleasure, should be a Dragon's goal. Lily's mindless glee was a temptation he needed to shun.

She was watching him, he realized. "What are you staring at? Do I have something in my teeth?"

"Uh, no, no." Foolish thoughts led to foolish deeds – like gawping at his ward. "Sorry, I was thinking. So, um, you believe you can still follow the thieves?"

"I can't, no. But Ghost can."

He still had trouble keeping all the members of her Pack straight. "That's the cripple, yes?"

And suddenly Lily was in his face, glaring up at him, teeth bared – before he could so much as twitch. "You don't call her that."

Her Wolf, a small ball of fangs and fur, snarled at his Dragon. A comical sight, one that almost brought an ill-considered smile to his face. But faced with his 'Mate's' anger, his Dragon became a bus-sized wimp. A thousand times larger than the raging Wolf, it still cringed and edged away.

You dishonor our Mate, it hissed in his mind.

It made Casey want to laugh. Except that, faced with her anger, he too quailed. Even Wolves had their pride, it seemed.

Maybe... a lot of pride. He remembered her fury when her father called the Blood Debt due. The way she stewed when he, her chauffeur, drove her to her chores.

For Casey, pride was the domain of Dragons and spirits. Surely the lesser Shifters did not feel its pangs as sharply?

Or did they? Lily seemed ready to attack him, to hurl herself into a fight she could not possibly win. (Not that he would be mad enough to raise a hand against his ward.)

All because he had given offense. That was pride – a pride he could understand in one of his own Kind. If Wolves shared it...

Perhaps that was the venom that poisoned their relationship.

If so, he knew what offense demanded.

"I apologize. I have chosen my words poorly and given insult where none was intended."

Lily took a step back, still tense and angry. "Okay. Don't do it again, though."

"What should I call her, then?"

"How about her name?" the Wolf snapped.

"But she is…" How on earth could he point out the obvious, without giving offense?

Furious and defiant, Lily kept glaring. "She fights differently than I do, yeah. But the Pack hunts together, and we all have different roles. Ghost is the best at what she does."

"And what she does is…?"

"She hunts online."

A hacker? The usefulness of the handicapped Wolf suddenly came clear to him. "So, if we can learn anything about these thieves, she can track them?"

"Yup." With one last snarl, her Wolf retreated. Leaving his Dragon awash in ludicrous relief. "I bet these guys used a credit card. Most motels also get your license plate number. Probably a rental, but that just makes the trail a little longer."

"And you believe the owner of this establishment will give us this information?"

"Voluntarily, no. Not unless you've got enough cash to bribe him."

The mere thought of such graft appalled him.

Which, in turn, dispelled the last of Lily's anger. "Okay, can that idea. Clearly you're too delicate for the job."

Delicate?!? More like moral!

No sense in picking another fight, though. Especially not right after she'd calmed down. "I would be reluctant to use force against an innocent businessman."

"Good," she snorted, "because I would be too. Nobody's talking about fights, buddy. Calm down."

"So, what is your plan?"

"I'm going to go tell him I spotted a bunch of scorpions crawling through cracks in his back wall. While I show him where, you sneak into the office, and get Room 113's info."

"I am no thief!" he huffed.

"And we're not stealing anything! Or are you too 'good' to

do scouting?" As he sputtered, she rolled her eyes. "Fine. Change of plans. You Shift and sit on a couple of cars. When all the humans go crazy and hallucinate about gas explosions, *I'll* slip in and get our info."

The mayhem that would cause appalled him. "That's an insane plan."

"Yep. But you're too stuck up to do the sensible thing."

"Fine!" he snapped. "We'll do it your way."

In truth, the ruse worked – all too easily. The grizzled old man who ran the motel followed Lily eagerly. (More interested, Casey suspected, in her long leather-clad legs than the 'scorpions'.) Left to himself, he didn't even need Wind's blessing. And five minutes later, when Lily managed to escape the old perv's attention, he had their answers.

"Room 113 was rented to Eric Denver and his 'wife'. Enterprise Rental car, California license plate. I also have the credit card number they paid with."

"Awesome! Let me pass that on to Ghost and see what she can do. Say…" She eyed him from head to toe. "They got any food up at Dragon Monastery? Real food? Because I don't eat bean sprouts."

"Clearly you've never had good bean sprouts then." The horror that flashed across her face made him chuckle.

Lily joined him. "Hey, you actually *can* laugh! Wow, who knew?"

A thrum of happiness rose from his Dragon. Casey ignored the foolish creature. "Come on. I think I can find you a 'real' lunch at the Aerie."

CHAPTER 9

After club sandwiches, beers, and no bean sprouts, they both felt more human. And the results of Ghost's search surprised Casey with their speed and completeness.

"Credit card registered to Eric Denver – but it's paid by some company in Los Angeles. Nemesis Associates," Lily reported. "Ghost can't find out anything about them. Car rented in LA. Card was used a couple hours ago in Flagstaff, Arizona, at the Rodeo Diner."

Flagstaff? That was eight hours away! The thieves must have driven all night! "They're in a hurry."

"But to where?" Lily leaned back in her chair. "They're on the road to Cortez, Colorado. If this is connected to Rex Fairburn's mess, that's where things started."

"Let's hope that's their destination. With a plane, we can get there before them."

First, though, he needed to tell his Alpha what they had learned.

Miles Kennedy granted them an audience quickly. The honor of that speed was lost on Lily; the Wolf fretted over the smallest delay. Yet even she was pleased with Kennedy's surprise at their skill – until the Dragon's face paled.

"Flagstaff? You're certain of this? They've gone to Flagstaff?"

"Yes. Is this significant?"

Kennedy switched into Marakeen, the ancient tongue of Dragons. "This is grievous news. I believe I know where they are headed, though not why."

"Hey!" Lily barked. "English, guys. Rude as hell to talk in front of someone like this."

She had a point, but Casey wasn't willing to defy his Alpha over such a small slight.

And Kennedy completely ignored her. "The carving they stole was a gift from the spirits of the San Francisco Peaks. A sign that the bearer was a friend of that sacred place."

"Those mountains are only a few miles away from Flagstaff…" Casey murmured.

"Right!" Lily bounced to her feet, knocking her chair over. "I'm out of here. Meet you back in Colorado, bodyguard."

"Wait!" He caught her arm and earned himself a ferocious glare. "My Alpha may know where they've gone."

"Cool." She jerked free. "Have fun with that. I'm going home."

"Lily!" Dammit, why did she choose this moment for a tantrum?

"Don't you 'Lily' me," she snarled. "Don't expect me to help if you don't trust me."

"It's not that we distrust you. But this is a matter of Dragons and…"

"Then you Dragons can take care of it. Without me." The anger and… yes, pain in her face stabbed him, like a dagger through the heart.

"Ms. King wait, please."

Kennedy's calm bass halted the Wolf's flight. She paused, watching him warily.

Grim and formal, the Alpha rose to his feet. "Though it pains me to admit this, I believe my Flight needs your aid. Should you assist us, we owe you a Blood Debt, binding our Flight to you."

No! Not another Blood Debt! Not when he was so close to freeing his Flight from the duty of the last one!

To his bafflement, Lily sneered at this generous offer. "Screw your Flight, screw your Blood Debts. I don't want anything to do with you."

She would turn down a Blood Debt? A favor from the most powerful creatures in this world? Why?!?

But he understood. Pride. They had shown her rudeness and no payment – no matter how rich – would assuage the sting of that.

Kennedy didn't know her, though, and the refusal puzzled him. "Then why are you here? Why offer to hunt our thief if you care nothing for the good will of our Flight?"

"Because of *him!*" Casey blinked as the Wolf jabbed a finger at him. "He's my… my…"

Her what? Her bodyguard?

Her Mate?

Stirred by hope, his Dragon rose, gazing down at the angry woman with adoration.

We aren't Mates, he reminded it. *You know that.*

So did Lily. "He's my Pack! My Packmate… Packmate-ish kind of… thing. And the, uh, Pack hunts together."

"Casey Briggs is not a member of your Pack," Kennedy corrected.

The Wolf flipped her chair back up and plunked down in it. "Whatever. Jeez, you guys are dicks. What do you want?"

Etiquette and protocol had flown out the window. The

negotiation sputtered to a halt as both Dragons sought some path, some courtesy to begin again.

Lily didn't have enough patience for that, though. "Look, I can't help you unless you tell me what needs doing. And forget the damned gold coins, okay? I don't want one."

Not the soft words the moment needed. Casey sighed as his Alpha's temper frayed even further.

"What you want is not relevant!" Kennedy snapped. "The debt will be owed no matter what you say."

Lily pinched the bridge of her nose. "You have the crappiest way of asking for help."

Oh, spirits! He had to intervene before she drove his Alpha into a rage! "My lord, please. Allow me to explain."

Seething, Kennedy nodded.

"Lily, the carving that was stolen? Your father brought it to us. It's why we owe him a Blood Debt."

"So, it's the reason my life sucks right now. Got it. Keep talking."

He ignored that peevish reply. "It marks the bearer as a friend of the mountains – the San Francisco Peaks. Any spirit who sees it will welcome him or her."

"And Dad got this how?"

He actually didn't know that. Kennedy did, though. "Your father's grandmother was a respected wise woman of the Zuni. Some years back there was a problem in the mountains. My Flight tried to appease the spirits, but they turned away from us."

"We are still outsiders," Casey interjected, "though we strive for Proper Behavior."

Kennedy nodded and continued. "But the spirits recognized and respected your father's blood. He acted as our emissary. When he finished, they gave him this fetish so that we might approach them, even though we do not belong to any of the Peoples."

With no pause, Lily nodded. "So, it's the key to some sacred place. The thieves stole it – which means they can get into this place and do something. Probably some nasty crap. You can't, because you lost the key. But I can, because I'm my father's daughter."

Oh, she was smart! Casey found himself smiling fondly at her. Though he quickly wiped the grin from his face, lest his Alpha see it and assume it meant he had forgotten his duty to honor her – from a distance.

"That is it, precisely. Will you aid us?"

"Any idea what they're up to?"

"One," he replied. An admission that startled his Alpha. Casey hated to play messenger for the First Flight, but they needed to know this. All of them – his Flight and the Sand Pack.

"Finn Donnelly of the First Flight warned me that the Fangs of Apophis sought a relic called 'the Aegis.'" Kennedy's nose began to wrinkle – until he added, "It prevents Nemagorix, the Destroyer of Worlds, from coming to Earth."

"Destroyer of Worlds," Lily murmured. "Now *that* is a nickname!"

"I have never heard of such an artifact," his Alpha huffed.

"Neither have I. But I fear our thief may not be as ignorant as we."

Silence fell as they considered that threat.

Lily, as usual, was the first to break it. "Okay guys, I'm convinced. Sign me up. Stopping 'the Destroyer of Worlds' from earning his rep sounds like a good thing to me. Let's go find your thief."

Her promise wasn't exactly 'The Oath of Duty'… but it would do. Casey smiled as his Alpha bowed his head. "You honor us with your service and we, in turn, shall give thanks and repayment of this debt. Casey Briggs, Brother of the

Flight of the Snows. Will you accompany this woman on her quest and give her whatever aid she needs?"

"I shall," he promised. Honestly, his vow to guard her would require that anyways. But the Oath of Duty required the words to be spoken again, and he did not quibble.

Unlike his fidgety, impatient Wolf. Lily drummed her fingers on the Alpha's desk. Both Dragons ignored her as they continued the proper ritual.

From a pocket, Kennedy withdrew a gold coin. Casey took it from him, with reverence. "I entrust you with this, a token of our most sacred honor. When the debt is incurred, you will give it to our benefactor, binding our fates together."

"I understand and accept this obligation. It will be my…"

"People, people! Can we get going already?" Lily snapped. "And chuck that damned coin away. I don't want it."

Ignoring her was getting to be a habit, sadly.

$\mathcal{I}$n a decent world, Kachina Well would be hard to reach. A ten-mile hike up and over steep mountains. In that perfect world they'd arrive first, thanks to plane and Dragon-flight. Set up a nice ambush then settle down until the thieves arrived.

Sadly, the world was not perfect. When he parked their rented Jeep on the side of Forest Road 21, Lily stared at Casey in disbelief. "Seriously? There's a road a hundred feet away from your sacred spring?"

"Yes. I didn't put it here," he muttered through clenched teeth. Retrieving a backpack, he pulled out several small cloth bags.

As he did, she stretched her legs. "Please tell me that's not the spring over there, on the other side of that picnic table."

"That's it." Bowls, feathers, and a bunch of herbal crap she didn't recognize. Casey stepped off the road onto the edge of the forest. She headed straight for the spring itself, but he called her back. "Not yet. We need to cleanse and introduce ourselves. The spirit here is angry."

"Because of the picnic table or the garbage can?" They *were* pretty tacky.

"Both – and more. You see that mountain behind us? There's a ski resort on the other side that makes artificial snow out of recycled sewage water."

Recycled… whuh? Horror lit her face. "People ski in piss?"

"*Recycled* urine."

"You can*not* recycle that crap enough to make that okay!"

Casey shot her a grim smile. "The spirits agree with you. So, we need to be on our best behavior, okay?"

"Sure." Dammit, if that resort was one of Rex Fairburn's, she was going to have words with that Bear! Recycled… *yuck.*

The better part of an hour passed while Casey prayed, waved burning sage over their heads, and scattered cornmeal and an odd-looking tobacco around. She let the Dragon do this not-really-magic thing. The whole idea of sewage-snow still turned her stomach and she *totally* got why a spirit would be ticked off. Hell, she'd be pretty damned annoyed if someone sprayed urine on her.

And if they said, 'Don't worry, it's recycled!' I'd deck them.

Waving her to follow him, the Dragon finally approached the spring, walking with prayers and slow, measured steps. Supposedly this thing wasn't a Wellspring, like the ones the First Flight guarded. Casey had some long, complicated explanation for the difference. To Lily, it seemed simple enough: Wellsprings did stuff, sacred wells didn't.

He hadn't liked her 'translation' very much. She still thought she was right.

A second thing distinguished Wellsprings from sacred wells. Nothing lived at a Wellspring, so they needed Dragons and what-not to guard them. Spirits (apparently) lived in sacred spots and didn't like babysitters any more than she did.

Another point in this thing's favor, along with its very

sensible aversion to trash, dirty picnic tables, and pee-snow. If Casey could get this spirit to talk, she was sure she'd hit it off with the creature. So, she kept her mouth shut and followed the guy who knew what he was doing.

The spring of Kachina Well trickled weakly out of a crack in the stone wall of a small canyon. Its waters dribbled over a small cascade of rocks and formed a tiny pool. Lily wasn't sure if the spring had been damaged or if it was naturally unimpressive. And, well, she didn't ask. Seemed like just the kind of question to set off an already-annoyed spirit. Even she had to admit, though, that the 'water from a wall' trick was neat.

Kind of.

Be polite, she reminded herself. Her Wolf had already lost interest in the little fountain and was checking out the smells over by the garbage can.

Great. My spirit animal is actually a raccoon.

Casey's Dragon, on the other hand, sat at attention. Tailed coiled neatly around its body. Wings folded tight to its flanks. Horned head slightly lowered, a silent witness to the man's chants.

Hey Wolf! Check out what the Dragon's doing. We're getting ready to talk to a spirit. Why don't you come watch?

Because there was a day-old McDonald's bag by the trash can and that was far more interesting to her spirit animal than some well-dwelling... thing. With her luck, her Wolf would probably trot off in the middle of the negotiations to check out the piss-snow.

"From the west we have come, bearing gifts, to hear your wisdom," Casey droned. "From the west..."

On and on, blah blah blah. Maybe her Wolf had a point about the garbage.

A glint of sunlight on water drew her eye down to the well.

And down, down, down, down into the ground. Under those still waters, a stone staircase had appeared, descending deep into the earth.

Lily's jaw dropped. Her Wolf came loping over, now intrigued.

"Do you see…?"

"Hush!" Casey waved her silent and bowed. Above him, his Dragon lowered its great head to the ground and crooned a greeting.

A creature made of tar stood beside the spring. Lily could 'see' it with her Shifter senses, the 'sight' that let the Kinds recognize each other. Eight feet tall, with broad black antlers stretching out on both sides of its head, it stared at them. Two tiny white eyes were the only color in its inky form. A long snout, almost like a moose's, jutted out. If it had an expression, she couldn't tell.

Beside her, her Wolf's hackles rose. Lily agreed. This did *not* look like a friendly critter.

But it was polite. "Greetings to the adopted son of Brother Wind." Its voice was slow and deep, like molasses dripping onto stone. "Three visitors in one day. How unusual."

Yeah, no surprises there. She'd caught the woman's scent as soon as they walked to the well. Definitely a Rat. And one whose magical protections had worn off. About two hours ahead of them, if she had to guess. The hunt pulled close!

Casey explained their problem with a pleasant (and unusual) lack of formality. "The woman who approached you was a thief. The token she carried was not hers. She stole it from my Flight."

"You should have guarded that token. It was important."

Both Casey and his Dragon flinched at that accusation, and Lily felt her temper stir. Like they hadn't tried?

"She was a very good thief." Her bodyguard kept his tone low and reverent.

"And, it seems, you were not a very good guardian."

Another twitch… but *still* he didn't move? He was just going to sit there and let this oversized tar bubble talk smack about his Flight?

Well, she wasn't! "Hey, listen up, Molasses-Breath! His Flight did a… ow!"

Casey's hand closed around her wrist like an iron band. A *tight* iron band. "Manners!" he hissed. "Manners!"

Good manners were earned, not demanded. But, well, they did kind of need this a-hole's help. Fuming, she fell silent.

Molasses-Breath stared at her. She stared back. Her Wolf joined her.

A note of panic crept into Casey's words as he continued his plea. "The blame is ours."

The hell it was! Her Wolf growled, showing its sharp teeth. Molasses-Breath's own lips curled – revealing a mouth full of fangs three times as large.

As if that was going to intimidate her! Lily snarled back herself.

"Please, Wise One," Casey yelped, with desperate politeness, "tell us what the thief did."

"She came, with no greetings and no gifts. Yet she bore the token and, out of honor for it, we let her enter our home and take what she sought."

"Looks like today is just *full* of bad guardians!" Lily chirped.

Casey wrapped an arm around her before she could shy away. "Could you *please* be quiet?" he begged.

"What? He's a dumb-ass! And he… mmph!"

The Dragon clamped a hand over her mouth.

She was tempted to bite him. But, even in their human

form, a Dragon's skin was tough as nails. Last thing she wanted to do was break a tooth.

The spirit watched their struggles, amused.

Once more, Casey tried the diplomatic approach. "Great One, what did the thief take? Was it the Aegis?"

The spirit's jaw dropped.

No, it didn't 'drop.' It *plummeted.* It fell like a puppet's wooden jaw and bounced against the spirit's own chest. For a moment it gaped at them, tongue lolling. Then a noise, loud and booming, rumbled up its throat.

Laughter.

"HA! HA-HA-HA-HA-HA! AHAHA!"

The sound froze Casey into a statue of shock and horror.

Not Lily. She slapped his hand off and took a step forward. "Briggs, turn around."

"What? Why?"

She popped the button on her jeans. "Because I'm going to take a piss in his well. You think the snow-melt is bad around here?" she snapped at the gibbering spirit. "Wait till you try the unrecycled version!"

And, of course, the big doof *still* couldn't abandon on his 'manners'! As she started to unzip, he tackled her. Both of them tumbled to the ground, she trying to squirm away, he struggling to pin her in place. Back and forth they rolled. Her Wolf barked hysterically, frantically trying to bite Casey with its misty spirit-jaws. Meanwhile his Dragon stared innocently up at the sky, pretending it didn't know any of them.

Lily writhed, drove an elbow into his stomach, and kicked off a rock. He rolled, pulling her with him, they spun, and…

Plunk!

They tumbled into Kachina Well.

"ENOUGH!" Molasses-Breath roared.

Damn spring wasn't even deep enough to drown in –

though it did soak them both. They scrambled to their feet, glaring at each other, water dripping off their disheveled clothes.

"I am so sorry, Wise One!" Casey gulped.

"I'm not!" Lily shrieked at the towering spirit. Too bad her Wolf didn't have a physical body. She'd give anything to have it roll that garbage can down here!

A long black arm rose, pointing a fat tarry finger at her face. "WHAT IS THIS THING WHOSE PRESENCE YOU HAVE INFLICTED UPON ME?"

Casey licked his lips. "This is Lily King. Her great-grandmother was honored among the People."

Who cared? No way in hell Molasses-Breath was going to let her into his little Spirit Man Cave now!

"She is *not* of the People!" the well's protector huffed.

"Yes, she is."

"Do not 'correct' me!" the creature shrieked.

For the first time, even Casey's deference started to fray. "Her father is Aaron King. The man to whom you gave the token."

"I remember him. There is nothing of him in her."

Like a fist to the guts, those words knocked the wind out of Lily.

"He is her father," the Dragon insisted.

Molasses-Breath drew himself up until he towered, ten feet tall, above all except Casey's Dragon. "Do you think I no longer recognize the People? I tell you, his blood does not flow through her veins."

A high ringing filled Lily's ears, and she wobbled. Beside her, her Wolf's tail drooped.

Aaron King wasn't her father?

Then… she was no relation to her Pack?

Who was she? Why hadn't anyone told her? The bitter

taste of betrayal filled her mouth as she realized that her Pack, all the people she knew and loved, had lied to her.

The spirit's image grew misty and it shrank. "Do not approach me again. I will not speak to you."

Then it faded away, leaving them with nothing. No clues, no Aegis, no token, no treasure.

And no family.

CHAPTER 11

*N*othing went right from then on.

Dead inside, Lily still forced herself to Shift and track the thief. Duty kept her going; she was too heart-sick to even hope for a fight.

Didn't matter. Their enemy stayed a step ahead of them, all the way. The trail led back to a private airstrip. The same one they'd landed at.

Shoulders slumped, Casey banged his forehead against the Jeep door. "They must have left a half hour before we arrived."

And she hadn't noticed. Hadn't Shifted, hadn't checked for tracks. She was too sure that they knew where the thieves were headed.

Oh, they got some information, like the N-number of the thieves' plane. Ghost might be able to do something with that. But her and Casey? They were done.

Nothing left except to go home.

'Home.' Hah! Bile rose in her throat as she thought of Ringo's Spread. Her 'home' was a den of liars.

Time to go back and confront them.

Her father had a lot to explain.

OF COURSE, HER FATHER WASN'T THERE WHEN SHE ARRIVED. Lily got to sit and stew for an hour and half before he stalked through the front door of his trailer.

And he was already in a bad mood. "The hell is wrong with you? You got the whole Spread walking on eggshells." He scowled at her, trying to stare her into submission.

Like she wasn't an Alpha too, his damned equal in the Pack!

Rage twisted her stomach into a knot. He had *never* respected her! Never treated as an equal! Things would be different if she was her mother. Mated pairs ruled most Packs, male and female Alphas. But her father's Mate was dead. And her? No matter what he said, he couldn't stop seeing her as his little girl. A child, not a woman. Not an Alpha.

Pretty ironic, given what she'd found out today. "I just got done talking to the spirit of Kachina Well. *It* says I don't have a drop of your blood running in my veins."

Lily wasn't sure what she expected. Lies, bluster, denial. Instead, all the fight drained out of her father in the blink of an eye. "I see."

Slowly, on leaden feet, he walked over to his desk and grabbed a bottle of Jack Daniels. "Drink?" She shook her head. He still poured one for himself and collapsed, heavily, on a chair. "I *was* going to tell you."

Oh, that was rich! "When? When I had kids of my own? When I was sixty? Just *when* did you plan to let me know that I'm not actually a part of this Pack?"

"Stop it," he yelled. "Blood doesn't make a Pack."

"Easy for *you* to say!"

His anger rose to answer hers. "Yes, it is. Because none of

the Sand Pack are my Kin either. I was a lone Wolf when I was your age. Sand Pack took me in, made me part of their family. When their Alpha got too old, I took his place."

"So, *neither* of us belongs here!" Lily laughed, a harsh and grating cackle. "Is that supposed to make me feel better?"

"Dammit, girl, it's supposed to make you understand that there's more to family than blood. The Sand Pack is your family. They raised you. They cared for you. They loved you."

"They didn't 'love' me enough to tell me the truth," she spat.

"Because they didn't know it. That's on me. I told them you were mine and they welcomed you."

"So, who am I?"

"You're Lily King. You're my daughter." In the trailer's gloom, the touch of his Wolf's presence set his eyes glowing.

"Screw you, old man. Who am I *really*?"

He winced, a motion that raised a whirlwind of emotion in her aching heart. Vindictive glee... anger... along with shame and remorse. Her Wolf whined, shivering at the anger that simmered between them. "I don't know who your biological parents are, if that's what you mean."

"So, what happened? Did a stork drop me down your chimney? Did you find me in a dumpster?"

"In a way, yes."

Nausea swept over her. Her parents had thrown her out like garbage?

Seeing that, her father... no, *Aaron* reached out for her hand. Lily shrank away, and his face grew even more clouded. "Let me tell this right. You're getting your tail all twisted up.

"Twenty-two years ago, I came across a dying Wolf up by Pleasant View. No car, no bike. Poor bastard was almost hacked to pieces. But he'd managed to stagger up to the highway. Before he died, he told me his wife was in the back country. Too hurt to walk. He begged me to save her.

"I tried." He gazed away at the corner of the room, lost in a memory she didn't share. "Found the place – but there was no one there. Except you. Newborn baby, wrapped up in a white blanket and crying."

Oh, he was trying to twist this into some heartwarming tale, but Lily saw right through it. "Are you telling me a dying woman crawled off – *away* from her baby – and you couldn't manage to track her?"

Aaron faced her accusation without flinching. "I couldn't. Couldn't smell anything except scrub and sand. Not her – not you, not your father. Held you in my arms, buried my nose in your clothes… nothing."

Crazy, unbelievable… if she hadn't tried to track a half-scented Rat just this morning. Slowly, grudgingly, she began to believe him. Who knew what magic could do?

"Lily, I did everything I could. I buried your father. I brought you home and told the Sand Pack you were mine. And then I *made* you mine. I raised you, trained you, made you what you are."

Kind words. He'd never once given her any reason to think that he wasn't her true father…

And yet the bitterness remained, like a lump of coal in the pit of her stomach. Caught between tears and fury, she wobbled to her feet. "Maybe I'd feel better about that if I knew *what* I was!"

Then she spun and stormed out, ignoring his calls. Ignoring her Pack as they scattered out of her way. Ignoring Casey who watched her outburst, brooding at the edge of the Spread.

Screw them all! She didn't need any of them.

She didn't need anyone.

CHAPTER 12

*L*ily stormed out of the trailer at a high rate of speed. Casey watched her, his gut sinking.

Looks like that talk didn't go well.

Her Wolf stalked beside her, snapping at anyone who got too near. People scampered out of her way – from the smallest child to the biggest, burliest biker of the Sand Pack.

Only he was immune to those attacks as he drifted behind her. Her Wolf drove everyone away.

Except him.

A thought that left Casey uneasy, yet delighted.

His Dragon nudged him in the small of his back.

Talk to our Mate. She needs us.

No, she needs space.

Often, words helped – but not today. Caught in a torrent of pain and rage, Lily wouldn't hear wisdom in anything he said. To her, words would be an insult. A trick to distract her from the emotions she felt.

He would not do that. Her pain was justified. He would endure her wrath until she had drunk as deeply from that cup of betrayal as she wished. Only then, when she had felt and honored her own feelings, would he offer comfort.

To do anything else was to dishonor her.

His Dragon doubted the sense in that… but it relented.

At the door to her trailer Lily froze, tense with fury. Fists clenched and unclenched as deep, ragged breaths shook her slender frame. Then a stream of extremely unladylike profanities spilled out of her, all screeched at the top of her lungs.

No one paid her any mind. Casey guessed Wolves did this regularly when they got upset.

Still shaking with anger, she turned to face him. "I can't be here."

"Then let us leave. A few days away might do us both good. And I know just the place."

"You're kidding me, right?"

In the parking lot of Ancient Ways, Lily glared up at the resort with open loathing.

"No, I am not. It is easily the finest accommodation in Cortez.

He could not understand her newest anger. Ancient Ways was a dignified resort with every amenity a guest could hope for. In fact, he'd ordered several of them. Yet the first glimpse of it fanned the dying embers of her fury back into new life. "And that's where you thought you'd bring me, huh?" she sneered.

"Of course. Why…"

And then he saw it. The way her lips grew pinched. How she wrapped her arms protectively around her chest. Her wince.

Lily was afraid. And, like any Wolf, she attacked whatever scared her.

But what threat could lurk here, within the resort's gleaming glass walls and elegant suites?

Casey didn't need to ask; he knew.

A biker, poor, of no particular family… Lily felt she didn't 'belong' here. She feared scorn, dishonor. That those within, both staff and guests, would heap disdain upon her.

Which they wouldn't. He wouldn't permit her to be abused in that way.

"Do you know why I brought you here?" The Wolf scowled at him, suspicious. "Because you deserve it. You *deserve* to have the finest pleasures in life laid at your feet."

"Why?"

Because you are strong and wild and unflinching. Because you are beautiful, a pearl hidden in squalor. Because I am beginning to love you – and I fear you may truly be my Mate.

None of those thoughts passed his lips. "Why not?" was all he said.

Uneasy, Lily scanned the lobby for threats. "I'm not sure they're gonna agree with you."

"Just don't knife anyone and we'll be fine."

THE NAME ON THE DOOR MADE CASEY'S SKIN CRAWL. *THE Thunderbird Suite.* As if one of the great storm spirits would ever lair here! Yet he couldn't fault the rooms themselves. Two bedrooms, to allow Correct Behavior to be observed. An enormous 'living room', complete with a dining table and 82-inch tv. Original watercolors by local artists brightened the room's cool, desert colors. At one end a platform, tiled with red sandstone, held the room's hot tub. Floor to ceiling windows offered bathers a panoramic view of the wasteland surrounding them.

Personally, he liked something a bit more private. The manager had assured him that subtle tinting in the glass prevented anyone from peering into the room. Even if it didn't prevent Casey from feeling like an exhibitionist.

Lily skulked around the edges of the suite like a coyote *convinced* it was walking into a trap.

One of his purchases awaited in an ice bucket, a little red bow tied about its neck. With long practice, he popped the cork and poured two flutes of champagne.

"What's the occasion?" Lily asked as he held one out to her.

"Unless I've lost track of time, the 'occasion' is it's a Tuesday."

Her nose wrinkled. "I don't like this crap. It's bitter and nasty."

"The sparkling abominations that one buys in a convenience store are bitter and nasty. This is champagne. True champagne, from France. Try it."

Face screwed up in disgust, she took a sip.

The surprise that washed across her face, the delight, made everything worthwhile. He took a sip himself. Smooth, almost creamy, with only a hint of tang. A lovely bottle – and he sent a mental commendation to Ancient Way's wine cellar.

Sadly, a knock interrupted the moment. "Room service."

At once, Lily reached for a weapon – almost dropping her champagne.

"Forgive me," he said. "I took the liberty of ordering an early dinner before we arrived. It's already been a long day." Her hand still hovered over some concealed weapon, though, and he frowned. "I thought we agreed 'no knifings'."

"I wasn't going to knife the waiter." Then, in a mumble, she added. "I planned on shooting him."

Dinner was a pair of steaks, grilled to perfection. Nothing vegetarian for his Wolf, oh no. And he'd guessed – correctly – that no delicate little filet mignon would please her. But a big, rare, juicy porterhouse was just the thing. Lily savaged hers, growing calmer and happier with each mouthful. Rounding out the meal were a small pear and blue cheese salad (which she ignored) and an apple tart.

Little was said while they ate. But afterwards she leaned back and gave a deep sigh of contentment. "I hate to admit it, but… wow. That was pretty good."

"Many of the finest things in life actually *are* nice," he teased. Lily snorted at him.

Food and wine had robbed her of her anger – her one defense against grief. As they sat, sipping their drinks, she seemed to wilt. Sadness, not contentment, filled her.

Not what he'd hoped, at all. Time to move to his next present. There would be no brooding tonight.

"Ready for a bath?"

She scanned his face, perhaps seeking some hidden meaning. When she found none, she shrugged. "Sure. Why not?"

A dozen red candles circled the hot tub. One by one Casey lit them, letting the soft scent of roses fill the room. Nearby lay a package of fresh petals which he scattered across the steaming water. Smiling, bemused, Lily watched his preparations.

"Your bath awaits, milady."

Again, she snorted – softer this time.

"I will be in my room, to give you some privacy."

Was it disappointment that clouded her face?

If so, it mirrored the ache in his own heart. In the days since that abortive 'Rite of Claiming', Casey had grown fond of the crazy Wolf. Her bravery and honesty charmed him, even as the sleek strength and elegance of her lithe body roused his passion. What he wouldn't give to join her in that hot tub. To seek a true Claiming – this time with no surprises, no demands.

Duty forbade that, however. He was her protector, her bodyguard. Nothing came before that. Not desire, not aching need. A Dragon's oaths were the only thing stronger than its love.

Hard as it was, he turned his back on her and retreated to his room. He would obey his Alpha and honor her father's debt. No matter how much it cost him.

Five minutes later, he spotted the flaw in his 'perfect' preparations. Ancient Ways provided its guests with thick, plush bathrobes. But Lily's was in her room. His 'restful' bath had caught her by surprise.

He could give her his robe, of course.

Casey tested his feelings. Was this a trick? An excuse to go out there and ogle her? No. Not... exactly. While that urge certainly existed, he truly wanted to spare her a naked, wet dash across the suite. Besides, the waters of the hot tub – and its depth – would shield her modesty from his hungry eyes.

Her 'modesty.' Casey chuckled quietly as he grabbed the robe from his closet. *Spirits, listen to me! Thinking of her as some wilting flower. If her modesty gets imperiled, she'll beat the crap out of the poor 'threat'.*

Damp, hot air and the scent of roses surrounded him as he opened the door. "My apologies. I forgot to leave a robe out here for you. I'll place it beside the tub."

"Thanks."

He risked a quick glance at her. If he tried to walk up there blind, he'd trip over something. Probably end up toppling head first into the water.

What he saw floored him, robe forgotten in his hands.

Tokens of love and romance surrounded Lily. Rose petals floated close, some clinging sweetly to her bronze skin. Candlelight cast shadows across her body, enticing and mysterious.

Yet in their midst, she was miserable. She knelt in the

center of the tub, arms wrapped tightly around her chest. A pillar of loneliness and sadness. Untouched, not soothed, by his gifts.

The sight broke his heart. He had failed. A true protector would have shielded her from all threats. He had guarded her body with perfect skill yet allowed her heart, her spirit, to be shattered.

"Lily…"

"You can put it on the floor there." When he didn't move, she peered up at him, puzzled.

"I'm sorry."

"None of this is your fault. You've got nothing to apologize for."

He crouched beside the tub, between two flickering candles. "I'm sorry that this has happened to you. Is there anything I can do to help?"

"You…" Falling silent, she bit her lip.

"Yes?"

"Nothing. There's nothing you can do."

But there was. He'd seen it in the brief hope that lit her face. In the wistful yearning that touched her words. "Tell me, please."

"No. I won't ask you to… to…"

"No request is too great." His words grew rough with emotion as he sensed a path through her sorrow. "I swear to you that if there is *anything* I can…"

"Stop!" Pearls of rose-scented water trickled down her arm as she raised a hand. "No more oaths. No more promises. That's how we got in this mess in the first place."

"I don't understand."

Face pinched, shoulders slumped with fatigue, she wouldn't meet his gaze. "I don't want to be alone tonight. But I'm not going to ask you to stay. I know what you think about it and I won't…"

He caught her hand as it drooped towards the water. Raised it to his lips and kissed her fingers.

His Alpha, his mind… both swore that he sinned when he desired her. But his heart didn't care. It swelled with joy when she refused to beg him to stay. To protect his honor, she would embrace her loneliness. She would retreat, unloved, bereft of Pack and father, to a cold, empty bed.

If he let her.

Which he wouldn't. A Dragon cherished honor above all else. Or so he'd been taught. Now, faced with her grief, he sensed a different truth. Love was a Dragon's first duty. Love and his Mate came first.

"Look, Casey, I…"

"Hush." He stood, rising above her. Slowly, one by one, he popped the buttons on his shirt and pants. Chiseled stomach, abs etched with ink… as each button parted it revealed a tiny bit more of his body. Offered her hungry eyes a tastier glimpse of what awaited. Desire flared, burning away the gloom that had surrounded her.

Then at last he tossed his clothes and stood before her. Naked, his manhood beginning to awaken under her greedy gaze. If she had any last worries, they died, unspoken, as he eased himself into the hot tub with her.

Bubbling and frothing, the rose-scented water enveloped him. Casey slid through their soft, feminine waves to Lily's side. Candle flames glittered in her eyes and wrapped her heart-shaped face in their golden glow. No sign remained of his wild Wolf, or the ferocious passion she'd shown at the Rite of Claiming. This was a different side of her, one he'd never seen. Vulnerable. Thirsty, yet unsure. A woman who yearned for love, not sex.

He adored both sides of this woman. And planned to show her that she didn't have to choose between love and passion.

First, though, affection.

Settling on the submerged seat, he pulled her up beside him and slipped an arm around her waist. She warmed under his touch. Snuggling close, laying her head upon his shoulder. Her nearness, the touch of her naked skin against his body, roused his desire to an urgent, aching need. Yet he pushed back against it. Desire's call could not be resisted forever. Now, though, when his Wolf longed for comfort more than pleasure, it would have to wait.

Surrounded by swirling waters and flickering light they relaxed in each other's arms. Heat and whirling currents softened tense muscles. He could linger here in her arms all night – if that was what it took to ease her pain. Breathing in the perfume of the red roses, soaking in that sweet, floral scent, the day's heartache faded.

As it did, a change came over his Wolf. She shifted in his arms, edging closer, the soft swell of her breasts pressing against his chest. She nuzzled his throat, her breath tickling against his ear. Hands that had floated idly came alive. They sought his body. Stroking the firm muscles of his arms. Sliding across his chest to trace the lines of his tattoos.

Signs, he knew, that her mood had changed. The time for solace had passed.

Now, it was the time for love.

With a pang he slipped out of her embrace. The flash of disappointment in her face shaded into surprise as he caught her by the ankle.

Kneeling, he took her foot into both of his hands. His thumbs found the tense muscles on her sole and circled them with firm, steady strokes. Slowly she melted, knots unwinding, tense muscles yielding under his fingers. Lily's eyes closed in bliss and she leaned back, surrendering to this new, strange pleasure.

As she did, he raised her foot to the edge of the water. He

kissed a toe, his lips joining the water's caress and winning a sigh of delight from her. Shivers swept over her as those lips curved tight, sucking, licking. Sliding her toe in and out of his wet, welcoming mouth.

When at last he released her, her flushed face and parted lips brought him delight. It seemed there were some gentle pleasures he could teach his ferocious Wolf.

Low in the water he swept closer and her knees opened to welcome him. He pulled her close, his chest hot against her sex. The bubbling water lapped across her breasts and lifted them, an offering he eagerly accepted. His mouth joined the waves, kissing her nipples, nuzzling the curves of her breasts. With a sigh she arched her back, eyes closed. His arms circled her, caressing the slick, wet skin of her back.

Yet even as her breath grew ragged, he slipped away, retreating towards the tub's center. Lily's eyes opened wide with disappointment when his mouth ceased worshipping her breasts. Only for a moment – for there were other parts of her he wished to honor.

Buoyant in the steaming water, her body was as light as a feather in his hands. Cupping her buttocks, he lifted her to the surface. Head resting on the tub's edge she floated in his hands. Waves washed across her skin, sending red rose petals sweeping across her body.

Once more he bent to kiss her. His face slipped between her thighs, his mouth sought – and found – her most secret treasures. Reverently he kissed her sex.

Lily gasped with pleasure, her fingers clutching the tub's rim. Emboldened by that, Casey pressed closer. His tongue slid between the slick folds of her skin and she moaned as it lashed across her nub. Mouth and waves pleasured her. Sucking. Licking. Under their assault, Lily writhed, her head whipping from side to side.

He, too, surrendered to the water's sensuous caress. Jets

of water streamed across his body, currents that swirled along his cock. As his lover moaned with pleasure beneath his tongue, the water stroked him. Roused by her cries and the water's coy touch, his manhood stiffened. Swelling, rising as his own passion peaked.

With a gasp he broke free. For one moment they floated, panting, eyes locked. Then Casey drew her towards him.

Caught in the water's embrace she drifted in his hands. He drew her near, then deeper. And as her body slowly sank into the water, his manhood rose to meet her. With a gasp of delight, he drew her down onto his straining, waiting cock.

Eyes closed in bliss, Lily took him in. Damp and soft, he felt her surround him, engulf him. Her arms twined around his shoulders, drawing him close for one last kiss. His hips thrust, slowly at first then with stronger, fiercer strokes as their passion grew. Water splashed about them, echoing their cries, the waves rising higher and higher with their ecstasy. Her legs clenched tight against him as her body slid across his throbbing cock, her slick, tight sex sucking hungrily at him.

Shudders shook her slender frame as her pleasure neared its peak. Lost in the rhythm of that ecstasy he surrendered to the wild, unstoppable need that sang in his blood. Each thrust drove her passion onwards, higher, until with a wail of joy she came. Her cry, her fulfillment, sent him spilling over the edge as well, filling her with his sweet release.

Spent, panting, they held each other for a long moment. Cradled in the frothing waters, weak with joy. Denying the world and its problems as long as they could.

CHAPTER 13

*B*liss could be so very short-lived.

Less than a half hour later, Casey found himself brooding. Wondering how, yet again, his honor proved as thin as tissue paper.

Lily's singing echoed out of the shower, mingled with the sound of running water. Warbling some country song about trucks and men who did a woman wrong. Casey sat on the edge of a bed, toweling himself off. His Dragon thrummed with contentment, basking in the glow of making love to its Mate.

A 'glow' that seared Casey's heart. For as soon as Lily had slipped out of the hot tub, his doubts returned, full strength.

Oh, she needs to be 'comforted.' Why, let's take her a bathrobe! What could possibly go wrong?

His guilt, however, only made his Dragon snort with amusement. *Foolish. She is our Mate!*

No, she's not. Not until she says she is.

She says now! his spirit animal protested.

'Sex' and 'soul mate' aren't the same thing at all! You can want one without being the other – believe me!

105

Foolish!

One word summed up his Dragons thoughts, completely. Then, deciding he was too silly to talk to, it ignored his dark musings.

Leaving him to face the consequences of his deed. Half an hour ago he had been willing to abandon duty, convinced that 'love' mattered more. 'Love'. Did he truly love Lily King? Or had he – once again – been undone by lust?

Lily strode out toweling her hair, stark naked. At the first sight of her, all his resolve, all of his 'noble' intentions, wilted. To his despair, he felt his body stir yet again. And knew that, if she asked him, he'd throw his honor to the wind once more.

"What's wrong?" She stopped drying her hair, doubt etching lines in the soft curves of her face.

Oh, spirits, he didn't want to blunder directly into this conversation! So, he stalled. "What do you mean?"

She wrapped the towel around her shoulders, mercifully hiding those enticing breasts from his view. "Why do you look like you want to slip out the back door?"

"Lily, no." He couldn't bear to see that worry in her face. Before that pain, his 'honor' faded away, meaningless. Casey scrambled out of bed and swept her into his arms. Words bubbled into his mind, protests and promises to calm her down.

But in the end, words were useless. Instead he kissed her, letting the heat, the passion that still burned within him dispel all doubts.

She melted into him, open, eager herself. Yet after a moment she drew back to study his face. "Why are you so sad, then?"

"Because I shouldn't have done that."

"Says who?"

"Says my Alpha," he told her, his voice despondent and full of regret.

And, at once, she perked right up. "Screw him!"

That was his Wolf. Casey fought a losing battle against a smile. At the first whiff of a fight her spirit soared to the heavens. "I'm your bodyguard."

"Yeah well that idiocy is my dad's… my…" She swallowed hard, and her spirits drooped for a moment. "That nonsense is Aaron's doing, not mine."

"My Flight owes King a tremendous debt. I should not abuse his trust."

"Screw him *and* your Alpha," she muttered. "I'm not big into 'shoulds' and 'ought tos.'"

"I am," he reminded her gently.

"I've noticed that," she sighed back. "I knew you'd beat yourself up over this. It's why I didn't want to ask."

"You didn't ask," he assured her. "I chose. But…"

"Don't finish that sentence," she begged him. So, he didn't.

They dressed in silence then, each lost in their own brooding. Lily was the first to break the awkward pause. "Is your Flight mad we lost the thief's trail?"

"No. Honestly, I don't think my Alpha expected much. He always assumed he'd need to hunt the thief down, in the end."

"I'll give that N-number to Ghost. Maybe she can find us a lead."

Maybe. Casey wasn't hopeful.

Fully clothed again, she poked him in the shoulder. "So, do you want to head out for a drink? Not much going on in Cortez on a Wednesday evening but hey, it beats watching tv."

"We could, if you like. Or…" He drew a deep breath and offered a different plan, one that had come to him as they lay, twined together, in the hot tub. "Or we could go find the spot where King found you. Drink a couple beers. Pour one out for your mother, whoever she was."

He expected her to laugh, to sneer at his sentimental urge to honor her ancestors. Instead, she froze.

Risking her scorn, he opened his heart to her. "I know this will sound foolish, but spirits matter. Our ancestors matter. They shape us and the world we live in. To honor them is to bless the gift they have given us. Your parents sacrificed their lives to save yours. Perhaps it would ease your pain to honor them for that. No gift is fully accepted until thanks have been given."

For one moment her mask of confidence and bravado slipped. Beneath it, he saw a different Lily King. A woman in pain. A Wolf who felt betrayed by her Pack and family. A soul lost in the world.

Casey loved that woman. Wanted to pull her close and sweep away everything that made her sad.

Except, if he tried, she'd bite him. He knew that.

So, he simply waited until she recovered from the shock of that grief. Until, once more, she put on her cocky mask and gave a false, cheery smile. "Why not? Sure, let's do it. You, me, and Mom, sharing a drink."

CHAPTER 14

I
t was a kind, thoughtful gesture. That, in the end, meant nothing.

Far off highway 491, Lily stared at the parched ground. Someone – King, probably – had piled up a tiny mound of rocks. A wooden sign with 'Liliana' written on it was the only sign that anyone cared about this spot.

Lily. Short for Liliana. She was named for her mother. Something she'd never known. Her father had never talked about his 'wife'. She figured it was too painful, and she respected his grief by not asking.

'Respect.' Hah! Turns out the only thing she'd 'respected' was his lies.

The memorial looked like a pet's grave. Nah, hell, it wasn't even that because no body lay beneath the beat-up marker.

So, this was where her mother had died. Lily gazed about at the twilight desert. Why had her parents come here, so far away from everything? Why would her mother abandon her to the night, to the scorpions and coyotes?

Casey popped the tops off three beers and handed her

two. "To your mother," he said. "And to your father, who died trying to save both of you."

"To my parents." She up-ended a bottle over the little rock pile. Beer darkened the stones before the parched earth swallowed it up. Lily raised the second bottle her lips and tilted it back. Her throat wasn't quite as dry as the ground, but the beer still soothed it.

Her companion's beer remained untouched, however. Casey stared off into the distance, mesmerized by something.

"What's up?" She nudged him with her elbow. "Should I have gotten you some snooty little micro-brew?"

Ignoring her jibe, he pointed at a pair of low hills, black against the evening sky. "What's that?"

"Uh, hills?"

"No. Behind them. Can't you see the light?"

At first, she thought he meant magic, some weird Dragon-y sight that only his Kind enjoyed. When she turned her head, however, she saw it too out of the corner of her eye.

A glow. Faint, hidden behind the hills.

There was something over there.

Something that would have been the only sign of civilization to her dying mother. *If* the light was there, 22 years ago.

"I have no idea what that is," she whispered, feeling strangely reluctant to approach it.

Casey didn't share her reserve. "Shall we go see?"

And damn her, she couldn't think of a reason to say no, no matter how nervous it made her.

THE LIGHT CAME FROM A RANCH. MILES AWAY FROM civilization, it twinkled in its own private valley. Faded paint, decrepit barns, and a sagging gate betrayed its age. It was old.

Far older than Lily…

Casey forged ahead as she dawdled. Across dry earth rutted with years of tire tracks. Under the telephone poll with its brilliant light, bright enough to illuminate a mall parking lot. Up on the creaking porch to the front door.

Three crisp knocks rang out as she sidled up behind him. From inside, a dog's bark answered.

Brave critter! Animals could often sense a Shifter's spirit animal. A dog that would bark at a Dragon had guts!

The murmur of a television clicked off. Slow, shuffling steps approached and the door opened slowly. Behind it stood an old man. Wispy grey hair puffed out like a dandelion, he wore a faded flannel shirt and dusty overalls. On the far side of the room, an equally elderly woman peered out of the kitchen. One of hands stayed out of sight, behind the door frame.

On a shotgun, no doubt. Sensible woman. Lily found herself liking the couple already. They wouldn't hide behind their door, too fearful to offer aid to a stranger. But they weren't fools, either. Unexpected visitors could mean an accident... or a robbery.

"Can I help you, young man?" The rancher's greeting was cool, but genuine.

"I hope so. My name's Casey Briggs. This is Lily King, from Cortez." He didn't offer his hand yet. They hadn't been welcomed. "Twenty-two years ago, when she was an infant, Lily was found just over those hills there. She'd like to know more about her birth parents and we're hoping you can help."

The woman in the kitchen gasped, and her hand flew away from that hidden gun to cover her mouth. Her husband's face paled. "There was a baby left out there? Oh, Lord, we didn't know! I am so sorry, girl."

But they knew *something*. She could see it, in the tension in their shoulders and the quick, frightened glanced they shared.

"Could we come in, please?" Hands folded in front of him, Casey was a model of politeness.

"Of course!" Now the handshake was offered as the old man waved them in. "We don't know a lot, but we'll tell you what we do. 'Manda, why don't you get our guests some iced tea?"

As his wife puttered in the kitchen, he led them into the living room. Only the dog, a border collie with a greying muzzle and one blind eye, seemed to doubt them. She circled the edge of the room, growling softly. Dragon or Wolf, the collie didn't care. No one threatened her home.

That is a fine animal, Lily told her Wolf. *I bet in her day she was a terror to every coyote in three counties.*

"Have a seat. I'm Jeffrey Clay." Their host settled carefully into his Laz-E-Boy. "That's my wife Amanda. Dodger, hush!" he snapped at the dog. "Don't mind her. We don't get much company out here. She's got no manners."

Lily didn't mind the old girl. Who needed manners when you had that much heart? The collie settled down at the edge of the room, still suspicious. Ready to throw her elderly body at the two intruders if they so much as stole a cookie.

They accepted glasses of iced tea as Amanda joined them. Casey scanned the room, as fixated in his own way, as the dog. As if he'd find any threat here!

"Is that your son?" He pointed at a line of photos atop the fireplace. Each one showed a rakish young man with dark eyes and wind-swept brown hair. Skiing. Graduating from college. Posing beside the body of a buck with an enormous rack of horns.

"Grandson. Lucas."

Amanda's tea remained untouched, clutched tight in her hands. Lily wasn't sure why she was so nervous. Dodger smelled her owner's fear and growled again, bristling with elderly menace.

Before Casey could launch into some ridiculous 'polite' chit-chat, Lily cut to the chase. "Did anything odd happen twenty-two years ago. This would have been in the summer, around…"

"I know when it was," Jeffrey interrupted. "It was the night that woman showed up on our doorstep."

'That woman.' Her mother. Lily's mouth grew dry. "Was her name Liliana?"

"I don't know. She spoke, but I didn't recognize the language. It was all trills and lilts. Beautiful, like a bird talking." He peered at her, grabbing the chair's arms to pull himself forward. "Your face looks a little like her. Delicate, heart-shaped. Though her hair was white blonde. Fell all the way to the floor. Never seen nothing like it. And you got more meat on your bones. Not saying you're heavy, of course. But that woman…"

"She was like a princess out of a fairy tale," his wife interrupted. "Spun from moonlight and cobwebs. Jeffrey carried her in, and he said she didn't weigh more'n ninety pounds."

What kind of Shifter looked like that? A Hare? Or was her mother just some beautiful mortal?

"You carried her in?" Casey prodded. "Was she hurt?"

"Bad." Years later, the old man still paled at the memory. "Things was broke. Her arm, her shoulder, things inside her. Blood everywhere. I don't know how she managed to make it here. And there was something she wanted to say, desperate bad. Couldn't understand her, though. There was one thing she kept saying, over and over. 'A dan eye.'"

"What does that mean?"

"No idea. I thought it was her name."

Lily glanced at Casey, but the Dragon shrugged. "Means nothing to me either. So, what happened?"

The two ranchers shared a look, and the old man sighed. "She died. Right there on that couch you're sitting on."

A chill swept over Lily. To sit here, where her mother drew her last breath…

"Did the police know anything about her?" Casey asked.

At that, both of their hosts squirmed. "We, uh, didn't call the police."

"You didn't call the police?" Lily yelped. Dodger didn't like her tone. The dog's head snapped up and she gave the Wolf a silent snarl. "You just… what? Dumped her in a shallow grave out back? Is that what you normally do with strangers?"

Jeffrey held up a hand to 'calm' her. "Now miss, you don't understand. It was a strange thing."

"Oh, I get it! Sure, it's strange to have someone stagger in and die on your couch. But why the hell wouldn't you call the police?"

Another pained look flashed between the couple. Another bout of squirming. "You wouldn't believe us," Amanda whispered. "It was too strange."

Just as she opened her mouth to bite their heads off, Casey leaned forward. "We'll believe you," he assured them. As he spoke, he summoned the lightest breath of his Dragon's power. A light, green and eerie, rose in his eyes. "Nothing's too strange for us."

Shocked, they stared at him slack-jawed. Even the border collie fell silent, cowed by that show of magic.

Jeffrey licked his lips. "We didn't call the police because… well, there wasn't anything to show them. The moment she died, her body just… melted away."

The hair on the back of Lily's neck stood on end. Instinctively, without thinking, her lips curled in a snarl.

"Like snow," Amanda breathed. "Even the blood vanished."

"Snow would've left water," Jeffrey sighed. "But her? Nothing. So, you see? What could we tell the police?

That a strange woman died on our couch and evaporated?"

"There wasn't even anything to bury." Real grief colored Amanda's words, as if that loss troubled her deeply.

A hollow ache filled Lily's chest, as if her heart desperately wanted to feel something – and didn't know what.

"I'm sorry we couldn't tell you more," the old man apologized.

"No, we thank you." Casey rose and bowed to them both. "You have given us some clues and we are grateful."

What clues? The fact that her mother wasn't human? Wasn't a Shifter either, by the sound of it. No Kind melted away when they died.

Slowly she rose to her feet, following Casey's lead. A quick thanks, a glass of tea declined, and they headed out into the night. No wiser than when they came.

Eh, not true, she chided herself as they trudged through the sage and sand. *You got a meaningless phrase. 'A dan eye.' Congratulations.*

CASEY OFFERED TO FLY HER BACK TO THE CAR, BUT LILY declined. Riding him seemed too intimate. Instead they trudged for an hour and arrived at their car tired and dusty.

Her bodyguard pulled onto the dirt track that had brought them to 'Liliana's' grave and headed towards the highway. "I'll call my Flight in the morning. Perhaps one of them will have some insight."

That idea didn't give her much hope. From what she could tell, the Flight of the Snows shared info. If he didn't already know, she doubted his Alpha would be any wiser.

But she had a plan.

One she knew he'd hate fiercely. A plan that would humiliate him.

A month ago, she wouldn't have cared. His baggage was his issue, not hers. But now…

Now, the idea of hurting him stung. Casey Briggs was a snob and he had a stick the size of her arm up his ass. Yet he meant well. He tried. He spent his whole damned life trying to do the right thing and not upset people. Maybe that left him hide-bound and awkward, but… hell, that was no reason to embarrass a guy, was it?

Even if it meant she might never know who were parents truly were?

Lily wrestled with that dilemma all the way back to the main road. Finally, with a sigh, she surrendered. Curiosity was too strong.

"Okay, I need you to be quiet," she told him. Casey cocked an eyebrow. "I'm going to do something that's going to tick you off. A lot. Just let me do it, okay? I'll apologize later."

"Lily, what are you up to?"

"Pay attention to the road, bro." She pulled out her phone and dialed a number she'd kept but never used.

Two rings, and then a voice as deep as the ocean answered. "Hello?"

"Hey, this is Lily King of the Sand Pack. I'm trying to reach Finn Donnelly of the First Flight."

"That's me."

Beside her, Casey's hands clenched around the wheel in a death grip. She didn't know what bad history lay between the two Flights of Dragons. But, as she'd expected, her body-guard was enraged by the idea that she'd go to his enemies for aid.

"Quick question for you. Do the words 'A dan eye' mean anything to you."

"Adanai. One word." No hesitation, no doubt.

"What does it mean?"

"It's a type of creature. Not exactly a Shifter but related.

May I ask where you heard this word?"

She glanced over at Casey. The Dragon ignored her, squinting out at the horizon. "I think my mother knew one… or was one…"

"I know an Adanai. I'd be happy to introduce you if you'd like."

"Geez, thanks!" That was a hell of a breakthrough, and generous. To her surprise Casey didn't take her gratitude badly. He was too busy glaring the sky to death. Something up there was annoying him.

"I could put you two together on a video conference tonight, if you'd like to stop by. My Mate and I are staying at Ancient Ways."

"Small world. We're there too, in the Thunderbird Suite. We're coming into town on 491 right now. I'll be in my room in ten…"

"Problems!" Casey bellowed as he slammed on the brakes.

"What the…!" Inertia threw her forward. The seat belt engaged and cut into her chest as she slammed into it.

And then she saw them. Two cars crossing the road, cutting off their path to town. Six men with assault rifles, aiming at them across the hoods.

"Ambush!" Her bodyguard threw the car into reverse. Tires squealed on the tar, filling the air with the stench of burnt rubber.

"Ms. King?" Finn's tinny yell rang out as the phone slipped from her fingers. "Are you alright?"

"Down!" Casey bellowed as the first bullet pinged off their car.

Phone forgotten, she was already ducking for cover when she saw the true threat.

A helicopter. Rising, all lights darkened, into the sky with a pair of missiles strapped to its sides.

Weapons big enough to kill a Dragon.

CHAPTER 15

Somewhere in his heart, Casey had known this attack was coming.

Three miles back, a worm of doubt wriggled into his thoughts. A vexing, 'foolish' worry he could not shake.

Something hunts our Mate.

Edgy, alert, his Dragon sailed overhead. He might question its intuition – but the great serpent didn't share his doubt. It knew. It trusted. It prepared itself to defend, with a certainty that almost convinced him.

Almost.

Then Lily called the damnable First Flight and annoyance swept away any thought of 'silly' hunches. And while he stewed over her 'betrayal', the trap was sprung. Lost in his own foolish irritation, he was unprepared.

But his Dragon was not.

Adrenaline and power flooded through him. It breathed across his skin and, like a pond touched by winter's kiss, his skin hardened into a thick, protective shield. Not the full scales of a Dragon, but something few bullets could punch through.

Time slowed as the first bullets shattered their wind-shield. Throwing the car into reverse, he wrenched the wheel to the side. The car spun, placing him between the gunmen and Lily.

"Down!" he shouted.

But did she listen to him? No, of course not. Lily fought to free herself from her seat belt – not so that she could slide to the safest spot in the car, the floor. No, she was struggling to draw her gun. Some ridiculous little .357. A pea-shooter in this fight.

"Get *down!*" Risky though it was, he took one hand off the wheel and shoved her head down.

As he did, her window exploded. Another car had pulled up behind them. Now it straddled the road, a shooter leaning out its window. Bullets ricocheted off his arm, leaving welts that would sting for days. Ones that would have shattered Lily's skull.

The worst threat – the helicopter and its Hellfire missiles – hovered overhead. Casey wasn't sure why it hadn't fired, but he didn't have time to worry about that.

Road blocked forward and behind. That left only one option: off road.

He flipped the car into drive and floored the gas. The sedan plunged off the highway and barreled through the rocky scrubland. Rocks pinged violently off its undercarriage and it rocked from side to side as its poor, delicate tires ground their way over sharp stones were never meant to handle.

Behind them, the gunmen scrambled back into their cars. He'd bought them a couple of seconds…

Or not. Suddenly the land around them lit up like a fair-ground. The helicopter pinned a spotlight on them, giving them no chance to escape their pursuers.

Yet still it didn't fire.

He glanced over at Lily. The size, the enormity of this assault had stunned even his wild Wolf. Pale, wide-eyed, she took deep breaths. With each one, she grew calmer, surer.

She's preparing to die. To go down fighting, even if the odds are impossible.

Casey loved her for that.

And he had absolutely no intention of letting anyone hurt her.

Even he, though, had to admit that the odds were grim. With the chopper pinning them down he had no chance to get lost in the desert night. His car, with its low clearance, would bottom out long before his pursuers' vehicles. And, frankly, the chopper could take them out any time it wanted.

What the hell was he supposed to do?

Fight! his Dragon roared. Images filled his mind. Leaping from the metal prison of this car and Shifting. Throwing himself into the sky and sinking fang and claw into that helicopter. Then, as it fell flaming from the air, turning upon the cars behind them with flames boiling from his maw.

That! Do that!

And if they hit me with one of those missiles before I reach them?

The question meant nothing to his Dragon. The supreme predator of this world, it feared nothing. Threats were a strange, alien concept. It brushed aside his question like a buzzing gnat.

Unlike his Shifter spirit, Casey knew that man was the true apex predator of Earth. Even a Dragon had to respect their destructive power.

If I don't dodge that missile, Lily dies. If I abandon her in this car it could roll and kill her. If it takes me too long to destroy that chopper, the others catch up and shoot her.

Lily is what matters. Not destroying our enemies.

Even in the depths of its murderous rage, that thought

pierced through scales to reach his Dragon's heart.

Our Mate. We must guard our Mate.

That maddening need to attack finally dimmed, letting Casey turn his full attention to their problem. They needed to escape, and he could only think of one way to do it.

A miserable, pathetic plan that might well kill Lily.

But what other choice did he have?

He glanced over at her, hunched on the floor. "Do you trust me?"

"Yes." No hesitation, no fear.

"Then scoot up here beside me. I'm about to do something insane."

She scrambled onto the seat and slid over, pressing her lithe body against his. Casey wrapped an arm tightly around her and felt her heart hammering. With his other hand he clicked open his door, letting the sedan blunder along its own path through the desert.

"Oh hell," she whispered, staring through the open door at the sand flying past. "We jumping?"

"Yup. Hold onto me as tight as you can. Keep your head tucked against my chest. And – if we survive this – don't move."

"But..."

"Trust me, okay?"

"Okay." For once, there was no argument. Slender arms wove around him and she pressed her face against his shirt.

Then he spun, turning his back to the door, and kicked off as hard as he could. They flew through the door, Lily clutched to his heart, as the car rumbled off into the night.

One second of flight, his Wolf held tight. Then they slammed into the ground.

Casey landed on his back, taking the brunt of the impact. Cloth ripped, his jacket shredded. But beneath lay a Dragon's scales – a shield no mere rock could pierce. The force sent them bouncing across the desert. He held her close, the woman he loved. Arm cradling her body. Hand covering her head. Legs wrapped around her so that the stones and scrub they tumbled through tore futilely at him, not her.

Yet even his protection wasn't perfect. He felt her gasp as their landing jolted her down to her bones. Heard her hiss with pain as the rocks tore at her hands. Still, he blessed her choice of fashion. Those motorcycle leathers she always wore were the next best thing to armor. Rocks scuffed them, thorns broke against them. And when they stopped rolling, Lily still breathed. His Mate was bruised, shaken, and scratched – but alive.

Now to keep her that way.

With no foot on the gas, the sedan was already rumbling to a halt. The chopper hadn't missed his trick. It banked and swept back towards them. Once more that light sought them, to reveal them to their pursuers.

Despite her promise, Lily squirmed. For a Wolf, the urge to flee was too strong. Casey held her tight and spoke.

"Brother Wind, hear your Kin! Cover me with your cloak, though I lie pinned on the ground!"

He wasn't sure the spirits of the air would hear him, down here so far beneath their heights. Or that they'd listen to him in this form. Wind was the brother of Dragons, not men.

A breeze eddied about them, swirling the dust.

Chance? Or a sign that the spirits favored him?

No way to tell. Nothing to do now, except pray.

"Casey…" Lily wiggled against him. "We need to…"

"Hush," he breathed in her ear. "Don't move. Don't speak."

The spotlight swept over them, lighting the ground around them with its harsh brilliance. His breath caught in his throat. He'd failed. Brother Wind hid Dragons from mortal eyes, not Shifters.

Then the beam flickered past, flailing left and right across the badlands.

As if the pilot couldn't see them.

Lily gasped softly as she realized what he'd done. Wind's Blessing was 'meant' to hide a Dragon from the view of the mortals it might traumatize. Casey never thought to use it to hide himself. And he still wasn't sure it would cover Lily.

Only time would tell.

Cars shot past them to circle his idling sedan. He and Lily lay, locked in a nervous embrace, as shouts and shots rang out around the empty car.

Minutes passed as their enemies ranged out, seeking any sign of them. Overhead the chopper circled endlessly, its spotlight probing every nook and cranny. A dozen times it swept over them. Each time Casey caught his breath, sure they were doomed. Yet each time it passed blindly onwards.

Warm and safe in his arms, Lily waited. Trusting him and his plan.

The search slowed. Angry, frustrated, their enemies snarled at each other. Over walkie talkies, pilot and drivers blamed each other for this failure. In the end, with no clues, they gave up. Engines revved to life and the little convoy headed back to the road.

Success! Wrapped in Brother Wind's invisibility, Casey grinned.

Until he noticed that one of the cars was headed straight towards them.

No! No, no, no! Sweat broke out on his forehead. Freedom was so close!

But there was no mistake: the car headed straight for them!

Try to roll between the tires? Hope for the best?

No, either of those things might kill Lily. Casey tensed as the car approached and, at the last moment, rolled to the side and prayed that either Brother Wind or the darkness of night would protect them.

This time, his prayers failed.

A shout brought the car screeching to a halt, horn blaring. At once the chopper whipped around and that damnable light stabbed through the gloom. Revealing the couple for all to see.

Fight!

This time, Casey had no other plan. His Dragon was right.

Time to see how fast he could dodge a Hellfire missile.

"Run!" he shouted to Lily as he rolled to his feet. Even if he died in this charge, he could buy her enough time to escape.

Doors flew open, spilling gun-wielding men into the night. His Dragon's power flared in his heart and he Shifted, rearing up to the heavens as great black wings erupted into the darkness.

Two tiny red lights appeared on the missiles.

Too soon! He was still changing, Shifting, growing, when…

A blast of liquid fire scorched down from the sky, wrapping the helicopter in its deadly embrace. With a bone-rattling 'BOOM!' the chopper exploded. Shrapnel and flaming debris rained down across the desert.

In the flash Casey saw his ally: a great white Dragon, its scales etched with countless scars. It swept low, scattering the gunmen before it.

Donnelly. Oh hell. He was going to owe a favor to those fools in the First Flight.

Time to worry about that later. For now, Casey launched himself into the air to help mopping up their enemies.

One Dragon they'd prepared for.

Two was too many.

CHAPTER 16

*L*ily didn't need to see Bree Donnelly's Hare to know what kind of Shifter she was. The leggy red-head's nose twitched continually as she stared at the bruises rising on the Wolf's arms. "Are you sure you don't to go to the hospital?"

"Nah. I've taken worse spills on my Harley. I'll have Bone-Dog check me out when I go home."

What *really* fascinated her was the line of fire-trucks and police cars flying up Route 491. From the Donnellys' room at Ancient Ways, she had a great view of the official hysteria their battle had raised. "We're gonna be the lead story on the news at 11:00!"

Bree sighed and cast a tired glance at the suite's living room, where the two Dragons sat, stiffly polite, sipping whiskey. "Yes. No one's ever accused my husband of being delicate or discreet."

"Hey, they're the ones who brought the missiles and the chopper!"

"True. Things like this always leave such a mess to clean up, though."

"Which is why I called my Alpha!" Finn interrupted. "That's what they're here for: cleaning up messes!"

Lily snickered. "Your Flights must be different from our Packs, then, because with Wolves, that's the Omega's job."

Casey joined the two women at the window. "We did incinerate our rental. Hopefully that will prevent the authorities from tracing this back to us."

And – also hopefully – it wouldn't set the whole county ablaze.

Dragons were powerful… but they were *not* subtle.

Finn wandered over as well and held out a scrap of paper. "Tess Morland's number. Too bad she was out tonight. I think you guys will hit it off. You've got similar tastes in clothes and bikes."

And they were both linked to these 'Adanai'. Faeries. The word still made Lily's nose wrinkled. At least these 'faeries' weren't glitter-coated mosquitos like Tinkerbell. More like Lord of the Rings elves with a bad attitude.

The four of them sipped their drinks and watched the stream of first responders flying past. "These were the Fangs of Apophis, right?" Lily asked the scarred man.

"I'd guess so, yes. No one else I know could produce that kind of firepower. Unless you've ticked off some drug cartel?"

"Nope." The whiskey burned its way down her throat, soothing the aches that filled her body. "I still don't understand why these Fangs didn't use their missiles at the start. It's like they weren't really trying to kill me."

Casey puffed up at once. Probably thought she was casting shade on his bodyguard skills. "Are you kidding? Those bullets were real. Any one of them would have killed you."

"Then why not use a missile? It's like they wanted to kill

me… but not too much. Like *dead* but not *so* dead that you have to have a closed casket at the funeral, you know?"

The men chuckled but Bree pursed her lips. "Could it be your necklace?" That cut the laughter short. "Sorry, I couldn't help but notice that it's magical and we know the Fangs collect ancient artifacts. Maybe they don't care if you die or not. Killing you is just the easiest way to get your necklace."

Lily's face lit up and she gazed at the Hare with new respect. It all made sense. "So, they brought Hellfire missiles to handle the Dragon. But they didn't want to use them on me because that would obliterate the necklace."

Finn kissed the Hare on the cheek. "Have I ever told you how much I love having a smart wife?"

"You have. Repeatedly," Bree replied with a kiss of her own. "Lily, do you know where the necklace comes from?"

"I used to think I did." The admission brought a sour curl to her lips. "My father told me it belonged to my mother. But, well, that's a lie."

"Not necessarily." The Hare's gentle disagreement smoothed the edge off her anger. "I bet it *is* some Adanai artifact. He probably found it with you in the desert. What does it do?"

"Helps me track things. Don't know if this matters or not, but it doesn't Shift with me. And do *not* call it a dog collar," she added, shooting the Dragons a hard stare. Behind her, her Wolf pranced, tail in the air, letting everyone know that she was teasing.

"Wouldn't dream of it," Finn assured her. She *knew* Casey knew better.

Her bodyguard was too lost in thought to rise to her joke. "There's something we're missing. I've seen Lily track and yes, that necklace lets her do astounding things. But the Fangs have launched two major assaults recently."

"And a half dozen smaller ones before that," she admitted. "That's why Dad was so keen to call in his debt."

Doubt filled Casey's face as he studied her. "Is a tracking necklace truly worth that much to them? Or is there more to it?"

"Well we talked to the Hares in Sedona and they didn't know anything. Maybe you've got an idea?" she asked Bree.

"Sorry, no. I'm pretty new to all this Shifting stuff and I'm not a well-trained Witch. If that Warren doesn't know…"

"We're kinda screwed?"

"Yeah."

Not much for it, then. Lily set her tumbler down and poked Casey. "Want to head back to the Spread and call it a night? It's early, but I'm beat."

"Sure."

Halfway across the room, her bodyguard slowed. Glancing back, she noticed his Adam's apple bobbing, like he was trying his damnedest not to throw up. "Finn Donnelly…" With a deep wince, he turned to face the other Dragon. "Warrior of the First Flight and traveler through the Lands of Snow and Sand…"

"Uh oh," she interrupted. "You're in trouble now, bro. He's getting all formal."

"Lily!" Annoyed, he glowered at her as the Donnellys chuckled. "This is a matter of honor!"

Finn waved his hand. "Don't worry, I got this." Facing the black Dragon squarely, he simply said, "Happy to help."

"But…"

"Don't mention it."

"Yet it *must* be addressed! You may well have saved my life. And, more importantly, the life of the woman I am sworn to protect." From a pocket he drew that gold coin. The one *she* was supposed to get after Kachina Well (if Molasses-Breath hadn't been such an a-hole).

The other Dragon recognized it, immediately. "Put that damned thing away."

"A debt of blood lies between us…"

"Look, just say 'thanks' and we can call it even."

"No." Somber and unsmiling, Casey stood at woeful attention. "Debts such as these cannot be whisked away with mere words."

"Uh, yeah they can." Lily edged closer to him and poked him with her elbow. "People help each other all the time. 'Thanks' goes a long way."

"We're not people. We're Dragons."

Like she'd forgotten that? Before she could argue, though, Finn interrupted. "Hey, I've got an idea. You can 'repay' me by forgiving me for all the stupid crap Owen Jackson said up at Lake Tahoe."

"Who's this 'Jackson'?" Lily asked.

"One of my Flight-brothers. A couple decades ago, our two Flights got together up at Tahoe. Ironically, the purpose of that meeting was to 'build rapport.' Well, things got off to a bad start. Then Jackson drank too much and started calling the Flight of the Snows 'Snowflakes'. And… things kinda devolved from there."

That was the source of the bad blood between the two Flights? The most powerful Shifters in America were feuding… because of some school-yard squabble? Laughter tickled its way up Lily's throat – until she saw the thunderous scowl on Casey's face.

Dragons were proud creatures. Better not giggle at the offense – unless she wanted to share the blame!

Lips pinched, her bodyguard studied his former 'foe.' "So, your aid this night is offered as amends to the insult given to our Flight?"

"Yeah. Sure." Finn shrugged.

"To erase the dishonor of all your Flight or just you?"

"Well 'all' is better of course, but that's up to you. The person who screws up doesn't get to say when the apology is 'enough.' If you still want to kick Jackson's ass, that's your business. He can pull his own tail out of the fire."

The big man's smile took any sting out of those words. Casey hesitated, then his ponderous frown melted away and he held out a hand. "Your apology is accepted. I will inform my Flight that you have shown us honor and I shall urge them to consider your aid atonement for the grievance between our Flights."

"And…?" Lily prompted him, as the two Dragons shook hands.

"And what?"

'Thanks', she mouthed at him.

Casey gulped. "And, um, thank you. For your help. I… appreciate it."

"Any time."

Wonderful. With any luck, this silly feud died tonight! "So… another drink to celebrate burying the hatchet? Or can I go to bed now?"

"Bed," Casey assured her. "Let's go back to the Spread."

THIS EARLY IN THE EVENING, THE SPREAD WAS BOOMING. Wolves danced and drank. Motorcycles tore wheelies, engines revving. Music, laughter, and occasional gun shots split the air.

Casey eyed the chaos with disapproval. "Perhaps we should return to town and find you a hotel room?"

"Nah, I'm used to it. This is a 'Wolf lullaby'."

"Hey, Lily!" Ghost shouted, waving her over. "You gotta see this."

The two of them trotted up to the young Wolf. "What's up, girl?"

"I just got a weird email from someone called 'Nemo' at Hotmail."

"Who's he really?"

"No idea!"

That was odd. Ghost was the finest hacker she knew. If she couldn't trace it… "What's it say?"

"'Kate Adams. Room 106, Navajo Motel. Tonight, or never.' "

She knew the place. A run-down strip motel with a concrete 'Indian' in front of it. Lily cocked an eyebrow at her protector. "Want to check it out?"

"It could be a trap. Plus, I thought you wanted to go to bed."

"I'm awake now."

He heaved a heavy sigh. "And, if I say 'no, I don't want to check this out', you'll go by yourself, right?"

"You're starting to really know me, aren't you?"

"Fine," he grumbled. "Let's go to this 'Navajo Motel'. Maybe we can make the news twice in one night."

CHAPTER 17

The Navajo Motel was the Desert Inn's tacky twin. Same crap, different states.

Something else was familiar, too.

"Bingo," Lily murmured to her bodyguard. "Our Rat thief is here. I'm guessing she's Kate Adams."

"She must be the person who sent that email to Ghost. How typical," Casey sniffed in disdain. "A Rat wishes to sell out her employer."

If she was the one who contacted them. Though Lily couldn't imagine how a thief, even a gifted Rat, would know how to get in touch with Ghost. "Well, let's see what she wants."

The Dragon rapped sharply on Room #106's rickety door. Soft footsteps approached, almost too faint for even Lily's keen ears.

When the thief peered through the peep-hole, though, her cry of "Shit!" was loud enough for them both to hear. As was the crash of a table being knocked over.

With one swift kick, Casey sent the door flying open.

Inside, a woman dove for cover behind the bed. Lily had

one second to scan the room. Chipped paint, cheap tv with a rabbit-ear antenna. Faded bed-cover stained with a dozen cigarette burns. Then, as Casey strode into the room, their quarry popped to her feet.

Holding a grenade in her right hand.

"Stop!" she squeaked in terror. A pin dropped silently from her left hand.

Meaning that the grenade would go off as soon as she released it.

Dead-man's grip. If she let go – by choice or because they killed her – the grenade exploded. The thief's squinty little eyes bulged with terror. "I'll do it! I swear I will!"

Grenades were the wrong threat to use against a Dragon, though. "Do you think I fear that?" Casey sneered, striding forward towards the shivering woman.

A grenade would only sting a Dragon – but it would splatter a Wolf all across the parking lot. Lily scrambled backwards, seeking shelter behind the door frame.

As she moved, a picture caught her eye. A wallet-sized portrait propped against the bedside lamp.

"Casey, stop!" Lily howled. Now she threw herself forward, frantically trying to grab his arm.

"Lily, no!" he roared, a shout of outrage that drowned out the shrilling Rat. He spun, pulling her into his arms and shielding her with his body.

"Kate!" She squirmed, fighting to free herself from his protection. "We're not going to hurt you! We only want to talk!"

That silenced the Rat. And baffled her Dragon. "We do?"

"Yes!"

The Rat retreated as far as she could, still clutching her weapon. "What do you want?"

Not 'Who are you?'. Kate Adams was well-informed.

"We want to know what you got from Kachina Well."

"She's not going to tell us that!" Casey hissed.

"And he knows it!" the Rat chimed in. "So, you better just leave!"

Sick with worry, the Dragon pushed her towards the door. "You need to leave. You're the only one here she can hurt."

"Wrong." Lily met his glare calmly. "Three little kids will die too. And I'm not willing to sacrifice them."

"Kids?" Casey scanned the empty room, confused. Even the Rat squinted at her in puzzlement.

Until she pointed at the picture by her bed. "Those are your daughters, right?"

They *had* to be. Oh, they were cute, like all children. But their small eyes and pinched faces betrayed their Rat lineage (as did their smiles, full of yellow, crooked teeth that would make a dentist faint).

"Yeah." Wary and frightened, Kate licked her lips.

"What's going to happen to them if you die here?" Casey's grip had loosened, and Lily pulled free. Though her body-guard hovered at her elbow, ready to knock her flat in a heart-beat if the Rat loosed her weapon.

"Someone's looking after them."

"The Fangs of Apophis?" The thief's wince confirmed that. "You really want them to raise your girls?"

"Not much choice." Kate's voice fell to a sickened whisper.

"Sure, you've got a choice. Help us and we'll help your family."

"Oh, I bet." Back pressed against the closet door, the thief shivered.

Even Casey knew what cornered Rats were capable of. Keeping himself between Lily and Kate, he edged back towards the door. "She's right. We know that the Fangs of Apophis blackmail Shifters by holding their families hostage."

"Help us," Lily urged. "There are Dragons that rescue these hostages. The First Flight has saved literally hundreds. Mostly Rats and Rat Kin."

The shivers grew stronger, shaking the woman's frail form. But despite their offer, she clung to the grenade. "How did you know where I was?"

No reason to lie to her. "We got an anonymous tip. Your name, this address, and a note 'tonight or never.'"

At that, a noise escaped Kate. A harsh bray, half laughter, half sob. "So, they want you to kill me. Save them the effort of doing it themselves."

"Yes," Casey said somberly. "Your associates have ratted you out."

Both women stared at him.

"Did you *really* just say that?" Lily scoffed. "Hell, next you're going to accuse me of wolfing my food."

"Er, sorry," the Dragon mumbled.

Fingers still wrapped tight around the grenade, Kate's arm fell to her side. "Well, I'm screwed. Anybody see the pin to this thing?"

FIVE MINUTES LATER, WHEN THE THREE OF THEM WERE SEATED around the room's wobbly table, Lily beamed at the Rat in amazement. "I had no idea you could put a pin back in a grenade."

"Long as you haven't released the spoon," Kate said. Matter-of-factly, like she'd done it a couple times. "Now, if you *have* released the spoon, you can still put the pin back in. But the grenade's gonna go off anyway."

"I'll remember that." Mentally the Wolf filed it away under 'Useful Trivia.' Who knew when you'd need to know something like that?

Casey cleared his throat and brought the two women

back to what really mattered. "Let's start at the beginning. How did you manage to break into our Sanctum?"

"I just followed instructions. Got a packet with a blue print of your Lair, its defenses, and the location of my target. Plus, an amulet that was supposed to hide me from 'Dragon magic'. Whatever that is. My handler arranged transport and all connections. I just did what they told me."

Casey paled at her words. "They knew that much? They must have had inside help but… I cannot believe one of my brothers would betray us."

"What about one of your 'servants'?" Lily suggested. "Morrison was the only guy allowed in the Sanctum. Me, I'd check him out, real good." Guy had given her the creeps from the start. Though she'd hate to think he was a genuine traitor.

Turning to Kate, she added, "So what did you get from Kachina Well?"

"A stone knife."

"Was it called the 'Aegis'?"

"I don't know," the Rat replied.

Casey shook his head. "No. 'Aegis' means 'shield.' A knife would make a poor shield."

Eh, good point. "You ever heard of something called the Aegis?" Again, Kate shook her head. "Where's the knife now?"

"My handler arranged a flight and this room. My driver Eric took the knife and told me to stay here and await further orders. When he really meant," she added with a bitter grimace, "'Wait for your killers to show up.'"

That did sound like the true purpose behind Ghost's anonymous tip. "So, another dead end."

Kate hesitated, squirming in her seat. Then she gritted her teeth and straightened up. "Not quite. I got a glimpse of Eric's phone when he dropped me off. He had his email up and one of them was a confirmation for a reservation at the Canyonlands in Monticello, Utah."

Monticello. Lily knew it. A small town about 50 miles northwest of Cortez. Just on the other side of Canyons of the Ancients National Monument – the place where Rex Fairburn caught the Fangs of Apophis summoning dark spirits of some sort. Looked like the Fangs had moved when Cortez got too hot for them... but not *too* far.

Grim satisfaction filled Casey's face. "We can make it there in an hour."

"We could. But what if they have another chopper with Hellfire? What if there's a Witch Hare there with one of those amulets that hide a person from a Dragon's sight?"

Of course, he jumped straight to the wrong conclusion and assumed she was scared. "You're right to worry about the risks. I should do this alone."

"Are you not listening at all?" Even the Rat started to smirk at Lily's exasperation. "All their defenses will be aimed at *you*. Not me. No group worries about a lone Wolf jumping them. A Dragon's a different story."

"I am willing to face those risks."

Damn him and his blind, thoughtless courage! "I know you are. That's the Dragon Way: charge straight at the enemy and destroy it with overwhelming force."

"We find that method generally successful," he sniffed.

"Unless your enemy expects the Dragon Way. Then you're screwed."

"What other option do we have?"

"Let's try the Wolf Way."

"Which is?" He pinched his lips, fighting to hide a smile.

That hint of disdain set her Wolf growling softly, but Lily forced herself to ignore it. "The Pack hunts together. We go back to the Spread and get allies."

He answered her softly, perhaps hoping a mild tone

would leech the arrogance out of his next words. "If a Dragon isn't strong enough to defeat the Fangs of Apophis, I'm not sure why you think a Pack of Wolves will help."

Fortunately, she was prepared for his doubt – and she began to tick points off on her fingers. "One, Ghost can find out more about this Canyonlands place. Two, Wolves are less obvious than Dragons and we can do recon. Three, Bone-Dog is a medic. If he's with us, we're less likely to lose anyone. Four, a Pack can surround an area – something one Dragon can't do. And five, I plan on calling the Donnellys."

Casey stiffened and his eyes flashed. "I will not beg aid from the First Flight!"

"That's why I said *I'm* calling." When he started to protest, she waved him quiet. "Besides, you're not asking him for help. You're giving him an opportunity to 'apologize' more."

"You do *not* believe that," he grumbled.

"No but hey, it's kinda true right? And tonight, proved that even if our enemies are prepared for one Dragon, two is more than they can handle."

He considered her plan. Nose wrinkled like he smelled garbage. "Why would your Pack help us recover my Flight's knife?"

"Uh, because these dorks tried to kill me? One of the Pack's Alphas?"

"Oh. Yes, of course." Even Mr. Snooty looked embarrassed by that slip.

"Besides, Wolves hate it when people do crap in their territory. Doesn't matter if it's 'summoning demons' or 'puking on the wall of my favorite bar'. People doing stuff in *our* places ticks us off. And the Fangs have been doing a *lot* of stuff."

He held up his hands in surrender. "Okay, you've convinced me. Let's go back to the Spread."

As they rose to their feet, fear returned to Kate's face. "Does that mean I'm free to go, or…"

"Sure." At Lily's smile, the Rat relaxed. "You can go if you want. But I think you ought to come with us. You'll be safer at the Spread – and I wasn't lying when I said that I know Dragons who focus on rescuing Rat Kin. I think they can help you get your family back."

Only a couple hours had passed, but already the attack on Route 491 seemed a lifetime ago.

One more fight tonight, she promised her Wolf.

Sleep could wait.

CHAPTER 18

Ghost was the first person Lily cornered at the Spread. "That email you got? It was a set-up. Fangs wanted us to kill this lady here." She jerked a thumb at the wide-eyed Rat who skulked along beside her. "Ghost, this is Kate Adams. I want you to check out the Canyonlands in Monticello – Kate'll fill you in on why. Then get her in touch with the First Flight. Tell them we've got a fight tonight and I want Donnelly here. Kate also needs them to rescue her three little girls. Got it?"

"You bet, boss!" For once, there was no teasing. The sharpness of Lily's tone said, without needing words, that this was no game. Trouble threatened the Pack. And, like a good Wolf, Ghost obeyed her Alpha.

Even Casey seemed bemused as he followed her to her father's office.

He's never seen me act like an Alpha. Probably forgot I lead the women of this Pack.

Of course, she *always* carried herself like an Alpha – a *Wolf* Alpha. 'Nip up, ignore down' was the Wolf motto. Unlike Dragons, Wolves constantly tested their leaders with little 'nips' of independence and challenge. A good custom, one that kept an Alpha on her toes. That kind of 'rebellion' would drive a Dragon Alpha mad. True Wolf Alphas ignored it, confident of their strength.

Then, on nights like tonight when crisis struck, the Pack fell in line with no hesitation or doubt. Days of constant testing had taught everyone their place and they obeyed their Alphas without question.

Time to show her Dragon how a Pack worked.

"Stay here," she ordered him as she knocked on her father's door. Poor guy was so shocked to be bossed about that he actually obeyed her.

"Come in!" Aaron King shouted.

His trailer still held some of the day's heat. Lily strode through the clutter to face her father. "We need to talk. Alpha to Alpha."

Quickly she let him know about the night's wild events. The attack on Route 491. Ghost's email and the trap the Fangs set. How she planned to turn that trap around on them.

At each stage, her father nodded. "They need to be taught a lesson about messing around in Sand territory."

"And with two Dragons backing us up, it'll be a lesson they won't forget."

Lily hesitated because she knew what she needed to say next. Even if the words stuck in her throat like a rock. "That bodyguard of yours pulled his weight tonight. I... don't think I'd be here if it wasn't for him."

Her father didn't gloat. In fact, he ducked his head, almost submissive. "I never meant to challenge you, Lily. I just know how much firepower these bastards can dish out. Dragons were the only things I thought could face that and live."

"Yeah." She still couldn't force herself to sound grateful but... he had a point.

Normally that would be it. He'd hug her, ruffle her hair, or offer her a drink and then tease that she couldn't shoot whiskey. All the things Wolves did to bond.

None of that happened. Instead, avoiding her gaze, he asked, "Tonight's attack. You going to be okay on it?"

Where the hell did that challenge come from? "Why wouldn't I be?" she snarled.

Her father wasn't rising to that challenge. "Because an Alpha won't lead her Pack well if she's angry with them."

That rebuke stung a bit, like getting whacked on the nose with a rolled-up newspaper. But was it true?

Lily probed her feelings gingerly. She thought of Ghost, her best friend. Of Bone-Dog, the Whitetails, and dozens of others. Her Pack. The people who'd raised her.

Her family.

That first flush of fury she'd felt had faded, and she no longer held any anger against them. "Nah, we're cool. No one knew I was adopted."

"Except me."

Yeah, that the one sticking point. Here she was, annoyed that he hadn't hugged her. Yet she hadn't reached out to him, either. Both of them stood here as stiff and formal as any Dragon.

Worst part was, she still didn't know how she felt.

"I should have told you," he said, his words soft and sorry. "But I was afraid it would drive you away. You wouldn't feel a part of this Pack. That you..." He swallowed, hard. "That you wouldn't feel you were truly my daughter."

All things she *had* felt... so his worries weren't wrong. A few reasonable words couldn't make the pain go away, though. "Blood does matter."

Ter father's nose wrinkled, as if her words stank. "To Dragons and spirits, maybe. But to Wolves, the blood that counts is the blood you spill for each other. Family is made, not born. It's made with love and nurture and the years you spend together. It's strengthened by the fights you face together and the victories you win. Maybe I'm not your sire – but I'm your true father. I raised you. I made you who you are. And I love you."

Dammit, this stupid trailer was dusty. Eyes stinging, Lily scowled at her father. "If you'd raised me right, I wouldn't need a Dragon bodyguard."

"Point taken. I'll be sure to fire a few Hellfire missiles at the next kid I take in."

She snorted. A grin broke through his stern frown… then she threw herself into her father's arms, burying her face against his shoulder. Letting the love, the strength of his embrace, comfort her. Its fierce protection melted her pain in a way no mere words ever could.

When the wild edge of emotion had passed, she broke away and swatted the 'dust' out of her eyes.

"We good?" her father asked.

"Yeah. Though there's one thing you can do for me."

CASEY ENDURED THE DELAY, COMPOSED AND SERENE – ON THE outside. On the inside, he squirmed with impatience. They needed to get going, *now*! The odds that their enemies would escape grew with each passing moment.

Yet he knew that every second that crawled by was time when Lily and her father talked. Father and daughter should be indivisible, each other's shield against all enemies. It broke his heart to see his ward feud with her family.

Let them seek peace. He would not fidget like some bored Wolf.

"Briggs!" Aaron King's shout boomed out of the trailer. "Come on in. I need to talk to you."

Both Alphas stood, side by side, almost touching. The

sight lifted the Dragon's spirit. There was a comfort, an ease between them that had been missing. This talk, it seemed, had gone well.

Casey bowed his head. "Aaron King, Alpha of the Sand Pack. How may I be of assistance?"

As always, manners seemed to amuse the Wolves. Both of them. King shook his head. "There's probably some special speech I'm supposed to say, but I've forgotten it. So, I'm just going to say what I mean. Casey Briggs, you've done your job. The Blood Debt between me and your Flight has been repaid."

"But it's not! The Fangs of Apophis still hunt your daughter."

"They'll hunt her all her life, probably."

"Then I'll protect her for all of her life!"

"No need. It's my debt. I get to say when it's paid in full. And I say it is now."

Welcome words. Ones that *should* have delighted him. They proclaimed that he had honored his Flight's obligations. That he had fulfilled the duties that Dragons held sacred.

But the words *stung*. They cut him to the core. They filled him with pain and rage so strong that he longed to burst out of this damned trailer and throw himself into the sky.

Because he knew what those words truly meant.

Lily hated him. She wanted him gone. Wanted it so badly that she'd risk death to be free of him. That was the price she'd demanded before she reconciled with her father: King must send him away.

"As you wish," he hissed through gritted teeth. "I will leave your Pack now and return to the Aerie."

Lily bounded to her feet. Behind her, her Wolf snuffled wildly, trying to figure out what was going on. "Uh, hello?

We're attacking tonight, remember? I assume you're coming. I mean, this is your Flight's dagger after all."

"I will not force myself where I am not wanted," he informed her, with icy courtesy.

"Who said you weren't wanted?" Her Wolf inched closer, sniffing at his toes.

That was it. Her fake confusion, her obvious lies… they were more than he could stomach.

"DO YOU THINK ME A FOOL?"

With a yelp, her Wolf darted behind the couch. Lily and King just stared, blinking.

Still they kept up the charade! "You despise me! Admit it! *That* is the true reason that you claim the Debt paid: you want me gone!"

King's bafflement only deepened, but Lily…

Fury sent her stomping across the room. "You IDIOT!" she screamed up into his face.

Casey reared back with furious indignation. Her Wolf stayed in its hiding spot. "How dare you…"

"Shut *up*! Moron! I'm setting you free!"

"'Free' to leave," he sneered.

"I don't want you to leave," she howled back. "I want you at my side – *free*. I want you to be with me because you *want* to be there. Not because you have to or because someone forced you. I want you to *choose* to be with me!"

She… *wanted* him? His anger, his pain… all of it came crashing to the ground as he struggled to understand what she meant. Lily wanted him beside her – in this fight?

Or beyond that? Did she mean something more?

Lost in a fit of rage, she didn't give him a chance to ask. "I'm a Wolf, not a Dragon! Wolves are free! We don't have servants. We don't take prisoners, not even from our enemies. And we *sure* as hell don't make prisoners of the people we love!"

That word tumbled out and exploded like a grenade.

Everyone in the room froze. Lily, stunned silent by her own words. Casey, unable to believe what he'd just heard.

Aaron King was the first to regain his wits. "Excuse me? What the hell did you just say?"

"Uh…" The two of them muttered in unison. King's Wolf stalked into the center of the room, looking around for someone to bite.

"Is there something going on between you two?"

"Um…"

"Well, uh…"

Wings beat overhead, whipping up dust devils outside the window.

"Oh, hey!" Casey yelped. "That must be Donnelly from the First Flight!"

"Yes!" Lily squeaked. "We should, uh, go outside. And greet him. And, uh, plan the battle!"

Both of them scrambled out, King's indignant glower following them.

Very few threats unnerved Casey Briggs.

Irate fathers, however, were one of them.

CHAPTER 19

The first thing the Canyonlands revealed was the social hierarchy of the Fangs of Apophis. While Kate the Rat got put up in crappy strip motels, the Canyonlands served a much higher class of villains. Beds of tastefully arranged succulents surrounded the motel, from the welcoming reception area to the sparkling waters of its pool, lit by submerged lights. Full blackout shades shielded the rooms from both the day's heat and curious eyes.

No Rats here, Casey was willing to bet!

It was also not the kind of establishment that would welcome a thirty-person 'biker gang', so the Sand Pack idled down the road while a kid checked it out.

Literally, a kid. To Casey's annoyance, the Pack had insisted on bringing two teenaged Kin. Twins. Two children… no, they were technically adults. But they were *useless*. Not even full Wolves! And honestly, he wasn't sure why the Sand Pack had come either. He and Donnelly were more than enough to handle any problems.

"The Pack hunts together," Lily growled at him, as if she could read his thoughts.

He was damned sick of that motto. "Those kids are not part of the Pack."

"Yes, they are. They're the Omegas."

"They're human! They're not even Wolves." He kept his voice down, despite his irritation. One of them, the boy, had stayed here while his sister did reconnaissance.

"Yup. And if they want to earn a place in the Pack, it's their right to try. Odds may not be good – but that's not my call."

Idiocy – like so many other Wolf 'customs'. No point arguing, though. It wasn't a fight he would win.

Besides, the girl was already jogging back.

Lily stepped out to meet her. "Anyone see you?"

"Nope," the kid panted. "No one's there except the clerk."

At midnight? Where the hell could they be?

"Clerk says some group rented the whole hotel for last night and tonight. Only about a third of the rooms are being used, but they took them all."

"So, we should expect twenty to twenty-five Fangs," King guessed.

"A couple hours ago, ten Hummers picked up all the guests. Then they headed north."

North. *That* was unexpected. Canyons of the Ancients lay to their south. Apparently, the Fangs *weren't* going back to their earlier haunts.

"What's north of here?" Donnelly asked.

"Whole lot of nothing," King replied.

Fortunately, it was the middle of the night – in the middle of nowhere. "Donnelly and I can canvas that area from the sky," Casey suggested. "The Fangs can't see in the dark and any lights should stick out like a sore thumb in this wasteland."

"Good plan." King clapped his hands and his Pack scrambled to its feet, ready to go. "We'll head out of town slowly. You let us know when you find our prey."

Locating the Fangs wasn't hard. Twenty-five miles northeast of town, they spotted an abandoned quarry lit with spotlights. So bright and obvious that at first Casey suspected a trap. Until he remembered that they had no reason to look for the Fangs here. He'd expected to find them sneaking back into those ancient ruins.

Circling unseen, high overhead, the two Dragons conferred in Marakeen, a hissing tongue not made for human mouths. "Tents," Donnelly rumbled. "They had twenty mercs waiting for them out here."

Heavily armed men who now clustered around two mine entrances – fortified by walls of sandbags and a pair of actual machine guns. "The important people must be underground. Why don't we drop on them? You take the left nest, I'll get the right. We'll mop them up quickly and head down."

The white Dragon drifted in silence, thinking. "What about the Pack?"

"They'll only get themselves killed. This is Dragons' work."

Even as he said those words, though, queasiness washed over him. Such an insult would enrage Lily. They'd come so far tonight, but this… this would hurt her, deeply. Could she ever forgive such a slight?

His Dragon thought so.

She is our Mate. We should protect her. That is what Dragons do.

His human half wasn't so sure.

Lily is proud. As proud as any Dragon. She'll never take me as her Mate if I can't treat her like an equal.

His Dragon shrugged those worries off as nonsense. It was a Dragon. *Nothing* was its equal.

Donnelly struggled with a similar dilemma. "I'm sure we could do this without the Sand Pack. But if we ditch them, they'll never forgive the insult. I need their good will if I'm going to work with the Shifters in this area. So, as much as I hate to say it, I think we have to let the Wolves decide."

"Alright."

His quick agreement startled the other Dragon. Before Donnelly could question his abrupt change of heart, Casey spun and flew off.

Secretly relieved that the choice had been 'taken' from him.

In the end, the plan stayed pretty much the same. Once more the Dragons soared towards the mines – only this time, a full thirty Wolves ranged through the scrub beneath them. A flood of silent, furry shadows.

Oh, and two kids pedaled mountain bikes furiously straight up the quarry's access road. Struggling, with all their might, to keep up with the Shifters. Casey prayed the battle was long finished by the time they arrived. He didn't want the blood of a pair of nineteen-year-olds on his hands.

When they reached the quarry, the Dragons drifted high above, like two deadly raptors. Once the Pack was in place (and just as those panting youngsters arrived...), he and Donnelly plunged down from the sky towards the machine guns.

His Dragon blood sang with a fierce joy as he slammed into his enemies. Men had only one moment to look up at their death, plummeting towards them. One second to scream in horror. Then they died beneath razor-sharp talons and a wave of liquid fire that melted bone and metal into slag.

Casey's tail whipped, sending men flying through the air. Bullets pinged off his scales. His head snapped up and another gust of flame incinerated that sniper.

Around them, the mercenaries scrambled for their weapons. But they made a fatal mistake: they turned their guns upon the Dragons, those armored killing machines. No one spared a glance for the quiet darkness that surrounded them. Until, with an eerie chorus of howls, the Sand Pack charged in, washing over their enemies in a lethal wave.

It was over. Oh, men and Wolves still fought. Mercenaries fired upon Dragons with a mad courage Casey almost admired. But the Dragons' first attack had snapped the back of the Fangs' forces.

Of their *minions'* forces, he reminded himself.

Their true foe hid underground, inside tunnels too small for a Dragon's bulk.

He caught Donnelly's eye and bowed his great scaled head. Immediately the other Dragon leaped to his side. As one they Shifted, down to their almost-human Marakeen form. No one would ever mistake them for mortals; their serpentine eyes, scaled skin, and fanged mouths betrayed their Dragon blood. But this form let them follow their prey through the mine's narrow tunnels.

Without a word they entered the mine, leaving the lesser battles to the Wolves.

Fifty feet in, the tunnel split in three. The right-hand path looked scuffed, so Casey picked it. But soon he hit another intersection. One that offered no clues.

Dammit, this place was a maze! How was he going to find the Fangs?

The answer came padding down the hall on furry feet. Casey cringed as Lily came trotting up. All the Wolves looked the same to him, honestly, but that necklace of hers was a dead giveaway.

And his Mate was *not* pleased to be left behind like an unwelcome child.

"Lily… um…"

She snapped at him, her teeth clicking shut an inch away from his hand. Then she gave a sharp, imperious bark… and loped back to the first intersection.

Where, apparently, the Dragons had taken a wrong turn.

So much for doing this the 'easy' way. He followed her, not looking forward to the scolding he knew would come.

A few minutes later, getting scolded was the least of his worries. This mine was indeed a maze, branch after branch of passages rising and falling. Lily galloped unerringly through it, nose to the ground. When the excavation broke through the wall of a small natural cave, the Wolf abandoned the artificial path and wound her way into the depths of the earth.

Images painted with red ochre dotted the walls. Handprints. Dots. Hunters with bows. Clearly the miners had blundered across something ancient.

And dangerous.

Light appeared ahead, reflecting down the stone walls. With it came the dull murmur of chanting.

Magic! The thought roused his Dragon's protective fury. Eager to shield Lily from that unknown, mysterious danger, he pushed past his Mate – and earned himself an annoyed snap as he charged forward, Donnelly hot behind him.

He burst into a low cavern full of Shifters.

Hares. Dozens of them. Most clustered against the back wall. Charms of stone and feather tied to their naked bodies, the witches groveled and chanted before an ancient painting: a twisted black figure, colored with soot and tar, whose red, staring eyes seemed to move about the room. Thick red ochre circled the monstrous image. But that protective line had been slashed, several times. Probably by the obsidian knife that the rite's leader held.

The knife from Kachina Well. What Kate Adams had been able to steal, because of his Flight's failure.

Ten men ringed the side walls, Bears and Wolves, mostly. Each one stood before a swirling spot of inky darkness. Some flinched as the Dragons burst in, but most ignored them. They simply stared, mesmerized, at that spiraling evil.

So many! Casey winced. With a higher ceiling he could Shift into his Dragon form and clear this room in moments. But trapped in this weaker form, the fight would take forever!

Well, at least he knew where to begin. Six Hares stood directly before him, at the entrance to the cave. Like their sisters they were naked. Unlike them, they neither moved nor spoke. Bodies contorted, hands twisted in strange gestures, they stood still as statues. Only their wide eyes revealed that they were alive.

For now. Casey planned to 'fix' that, though.

Bellowing a challenge, he sprinted ahead – and slammed into an invisible barrier as tough as a steel wall. Dazed, he staggered back.

"Magi…"

WHAM! Donnelly slammed into the shield before he could gasp that warning out. He, too, bounced ineffectually.

At the sound of his challenge, the Witch Queen's head snapped around. "Status?"

Stiff as a board, the Hare in front of him cried, "Holding. Hurry up. I can't keep them out long."

Lily, warned by their failures, hopped into the air – and kicked off that same barrier.

Pure, unholy joy lit the Witch Queen's face when she saw the Wolf. Spinning, she threw herself to the ground before the painting. "Nemagorix! Lord of this world! Behold! We have brought you what you demanded!"

A voice made of treacle and darkness oozed through the room. "You have only 'brought' me half of what I seek."

What were they talking about? Lily's necklace? Was half of… what?

That was a thought for later, calmer times. Right now, they needed to break through to their enemies.

Both Dragons threw themselves at the magical shields, again and again. Beads of sweat began to trickle down the Hare's brow. But her protections held, unwavering. And at the rear of the cave, the chanting never slowed.

Howls and padding paws approached and suddenly the Sand Pack swirled around Casey. Dozens of bodies threw themselves against the Fangs' shields.

And still they held.

Shudders swept across the circles of darkness that lined the walls, and as the Witches wailed and gibbered, those discs began to swell. A thick, viscous fluid bulged out and sent stringy tendrils questing through the air. Seeking the bodies of the Shifter men who stood nearby.

"Lord of Darkness," the Witch Queen howled. "Send your army to us! Join with us! Make our bodies the vessels of your power!"

"Oh hell no. No, no, no," Donnelly groaned.

Casey poured every ounce of his strength into his attack. With bone-jarring force he threw himself against the barrier, again and again, raising bruises under his own impenetrable scales.

But no force, mortal or Dragon, seemed capable of destroying this unholy magic. Casey gasped, fighting to find some reserve of strength within himself. Something, anything, to save the day.

Then Lily stood beside him in her human form. A pillar

of fierce calm amid the storm of Wolves and Dragons battering themselves against the wall. Turning her back to her enemy, she screamed back up the passage. "Brenden! Millie! Deck that bitch!"

Two forms shot past him: a boy and a girl. And when they reached that invisible wall, bane of their 'betters', the two Kin didn't even slow. They darted ahead and tackled the Witch with a force that would make any NFL linebacker proud.

As the three hit the ground, that unbreakable wall vanished. Wolves and Dragons spilled into the midst of their foes.

"Get them!" Aaron King howled. "Go, go, go!"

Casey needed no urging. Arms and legs pumping, he flashed across the room, straight for the horrified Witch Queen.

And then there was a reckoning.

A quick and bloody reckoning.

CHAPTER 20

To Casey, the celebration at the Spread was a raucous affair. Motorcycles screamed through shrieking, laughing Wolves. Some spun in circles, filling the air with dust. Others popped wheelies that threatened to spill their riders onto the ground. Everywhere Wolves drank, toasting each other and their own exploits. Their Wolf spirits streamed through the gathering, howling and wrestling. Brendan and Millie, the two youngsters who'd cemented their place in the Sand Pack, were cheered and joyfully pummeled at every turn.

Yet, sitting beside him on her trailer's steps, Lily gazed out across the chaos with a serene joy. Now and then a Wolf spirit trotted over to sniff her Wolf. Other than that, they were alone. A tiny spot of quiet amid the tumult of celebration.

One question still bothered Casey. "Lily, how did you know that the Hares' magic only repulsed magical things, like Shifters?"

"I didn't," she admitted. "But I figured it was worth a try. Powerful people plan for powerful attacks. Lots of times they forget the little guys."

He flushed at her words; he had treated her and her Pack in the exact same way. Yet no anger lurked in the Wolf's face. Lily was a creature of the moment, the now. What happened was the past, gone now.

Finn Donnelly strolled over, pocketing his phone as he stepped delicately around yet another snuffling Wolf spirit. "Bad news. My Mate took a look at that painting and confirmed it's a gate to wherever Nemagorix dwells. That rusty-looking paint around it? That was the lock. The Fangs managed to break it."

"With the knife they stole from my Flight."

Loyal and fierce, Lily immediately jumped to his defense. "Hey, guarding that knife was Molasses-Breath's job, not yours. He's the one who screwed up."

"But without our token…"

"All that did was let them talk to Molasses-Breath. He's the dumbass who lost the knife. In fact," her face brightened, "we should go back to Flagstaff and take a dump in one of his snow banks. Let him know what we think of him."

So much for being 'a creature of the moment.' Lily clung to some parts of the past with the tenacity of a terrier.

Casey tried to steer the conversation back on point. "I'll speak to my Flight. We'll see about purchasing the mines and putting a guard – mortal *and* Dragon – on it."

"And I'll get in touch with the Sedona Warren," Donnelly offered. "Maybe they can replace that broken magical lock." Inside his pocket, his phone chirped. The Dragon fished it out and a broad smile broke across his craggy face. "If you'll excuse me, I need to go find Kate Adams. Got a picture she'll want to see."

He turned the phone towards them. A slender man with ruffled brown hair and a rakish smile had sent a 'selfie' of himself and three small girls. Little Rat girls who, sadly, had inherited their mother's crooked teeth and beady eyes. Each stared at a plate of pancakes topped with whipped cream and strawberries. They might not win any beauty contests – but the joy and delighted greed that lit their faces was adorable.

Despite himself, Casey was impressed. "That was fast! It took what? Four hours? Six?"

"Private jets for the win. Plus, Kate knew where they were. She just needed a big stick to get them out."

And that's what Dragons were. The biggest 'sticks' on the planet. "Is that man one of your Brothers?"

"Yup. Owen Jackson."

Ah. The imbecile who'd dubbed the Flight of the Snows 'Snowflakes.' Casey's nose wrinkled.

"He used to be a playboy and a bit of a dick," Donnelly added, seeing that look of disgust. "He's got a Mate and a family now, and she calmed him down a lot. These days he spends most of his time saving Rats, not partying on the Riviera. Kind of my Flight's Rat Whisperer."

Hmmph. Maybe he'd changed… or maybe not. The Flight of the Snows would reserve judgment.

Lily was studying him, a faint smile on her lips. Alright, so maybe she wasn't the only one who could be slow to let an insult slide.

The big man headed off in search of the girls' mother. Leaving him and the Wolf in a comfortable silence.

It was late. The sun had already peaked over the edge of the horizon, promising another hot summer day. Wolves might be willing and able to party through the night, but a dull lethargy crept over Casey, calling him to the comfort of bed.

It was a call he resisted, however. Because answering it meant leaving.

Forever.

Nothing kept him here now. The Blood Debt was paid.

The Fangs were defeated. And, well, Lily had made it clear that she would never accept his Dragon's Claiming.

Nothing remained, except to say goodbye and leave.

And he couldn't do it. Couldn't make himself shake her hand politely and return to the Aerie. No matter how tired he grew, no matter how many yawns he had to stifle, he stayed. Sitting, beside her. Savoring his last moments with the woman he'd come to love. Trying to ignore three more damned Wolves that just *had* to sniff Lily's Wolf from head to tail.

Sadly, Lily didn't understand what the moment meant, or why it ought to last forever. She stretched and rose slowly to her feet. "Time for me to head to bed. I am beat to hell."

This was it, then. The end. Heart sinking, Casey rose and bowed before her. "Lily King, it has been an honor and… and yes, a pleasure to guard you."

"Jeez, buddy, don't turn this into some big thing. I'm just going to bed."

This is how he would remember her. Rumpled and bruised from the fight, yet radiant with life and joy. "I just want you to know that this was not a burden I loathed."

Still she didn't understand the import of the moment. "Uh, okay. Sure. Say, since you're not my bodyguard any more, there's no reason you can't join me. I warn you: I'm going to fall asleep the minute my head hits the pillow. But when we wake up…"

Her grin, wild and passionate, tempted him to postpone his fate. To take one last, deep draught from the cup of pleasure before it was lost to him, forever.

No. Lily King deserved better than some one-night stand. "I should leave. Return to my Flight. They'll want a detailed explanation of tonight's events."

"Wait." She peered closely at his face, as if doubted he was serious. "You're leaving? As in, leaving, leaving? For good?"

"Yes. As you said, my duty has ended."

"And duty was the only reason you ever came."

Was that pain in her face? Regret? He longed to pull her to him, but she folded her arms across her chest.

Now he *couldn't* leave. Not until she understood.

With gentle grief, he spoke from his heart. "Lily, listen. When you called my Debt paid, I finally understood why you rejected the Rite of Claiming." Hurt and angry, she said nothing. So, Casey spelled it out for her. "To me, to a Dragon, Claiming a Mate is embracing your destiny. You accept your Fate. You welcome it and it fulfills you, giving meaning to your life.

"I never stopped to think what it would mean to a Wolf. But when you set me 'free', I realized that you were still a prisoner. Claiming wasn't some joyous bond. It was a chain, a rope around your neck. Something you needed to escape."

"I understand," he promised her. "And now I, too, set you free. We are not Mates. I place no chains upon you."

Lily scowled off into the desert, blinking furiously. When she spoke, her words were rough with tears. "If you choose to wear it, it's a 'fashion statement' – not a dog collar."

If you choose...

All morning his Dragon had lain coiled, wrapped in misery. Now its head rose. Its nostrils flared as it scented the air, unsure it had understood...

Did she just choose... me?

"Of course, I know you're not interested in me. Not after the mess I made at your Lair. I'd be a..."

"Lily, no!" he breathed, shocked that she could doubt herself. "You are fierce and beautiful, wild and untamed. But I love you! With all my heart! There is no other woman I want beside me, at home and in battle."

"Are you sure?" she asked, strangely vulnerable. "I mean, I don't clean up well. I'm a hot mess."

"And I'm a cold fish, awkward and formal."

"Eh, you're not that bad." Now her smile stole back, impish and playful. "Once I got used to you, you're pretty funny."

Casey winced. That wasn't exactly a resounding pledge of love.

But her next words were. "You're also the bravest and most honorable man I've ever met. You care, about everything. Nothing – and no one – is too small to matter. You're hot, you're funny, and I, uh, I… you know."

He peered at her. She scowled back.

"Fine. Make me say it. I love you."

"Isn't it the guy who's supposed to have trouble with those words?"

"Well I already said them once," she grumbled, a mischievous glint in her eyes. "Shouldn't have to keep repeating myself."

Finally, the dam inside him broke. As his Dragon reared roaring its joy to the sky, he kissed his love gently. "Then Lily King, Alpha of the Sand Pack, would you marry me? Will you be my Mate, the bright half of my soul?"

"I will. And I…"

Another Wolf trotted up. This one stuck it's nose directly in her Wolf's butt.

"People! What the hell? Why is everybody sniffing me tonight?"

Her Wolf glanced up at her. Words passed between Shifter and spirit animal, a private conversation he couldn't hear. All the blood drained from Lily's face.

"Oh hell…" she whispered.

All of a Dragon's protective urges flooded through him. "What's wrong? Tell me."

"Nothing's wrong. It's just…" Another pair of Wolves

ambled over, noses twitching. "She says everyone wants to smell me, now that I'm pregnant."

"You're..." His jaw dropped. "We have a... We're going to be..."

Lily sighed. "I'm going to be a lousy mother."

"You will *not!*" He gave her a quick shake and a slower hug. "You will make a *wonderful* mother!"

"Well, at least we'll have the first toddler that can shoot her way out of the nursery."

And I would be proud to be the father of such a girl, he promised himself, as their laughter twined together.

* * *

Thank you for reading Alpha Protector Dragon! We hope you are loving the Shifters of the Aegis series. Following is a little preview of the next story in the series, Damaged Lost Wolf...

Click here to get right to reading Damaged Lost Wolf, available on Amazon!

Here's a little preview of Damaged Lost Wolf...

SUNLIGHT FILLED THE DINING ROOM. UNDER ITS TOUCH, THE cream-white walls burned gold. Sparkles glittered across the spotless glass of the table and the sandstone tiles of the floor. Neither dirt nor noise was tolerated here. The only sound was the soft hiss of the air conditioning, the lone defender keeping the Arizona summer heat at bay.

Under her mother's withering stare, Ash Anderson longed to melt away like an ice cube. Leaving nothing behind except a little puddle of misery.

"Am I in trouble?"

"You? No. *I*, on the other hand, have been reprimanded for your foolishness." Her mother's nose twitched, a subtle sign of her annoyance. Magdalene Anderson was a Shifter, a Witch Hare. Tall, rail-thin, with a crown of flaming red hair that trumpeted her magical power to any wise person. Her eyes, too, proclaimed her nature: one green, one blue, as with all the greatest Hare.

Ash's eyes were brown, like her hair. Short, with soft curves and a round 'cute' face. She hadn't inherited any of her mother's looks.

Or her magical talent. Which was the very heart of the problem.

"I don't understand why your Warren would be upset. It was a good paper, my Master's thesis. My advisors said that..."

"Your advisors are professors, *not* Witches, Ashbaline," her mother sighed.

Lord, how Ash hated her full name! No matter how much she begged, though, Mom wouldn't let it go. "Did anyone even read it?"

"Yes."

"And?" Resolute, confident, she prepared to argue. Her theory on the interpretation of Ancestral Pueblan religious symbolism was a startling breakthrough – which, to some people, meant it had to be complete lunacy. Ash had already been challenged a dozen times by fellow academics and researchers.

"And you completely failed to grasp what the Sedona Warren is."

That argument caught her by surprise, and she felt all of her prepared speeches slip away.

Folding her hands on the table, her mother fixed a sad, pitying gaze on her. Beneath it, Ash felt her hard-won maturity slipping away. Every time her mother lectured her, she became twelve years old again.

"The Sedona Warren is the premier coven of America, one of the most prestigious in the Shifter world."

That was open to debate. Ash could name three Warrens off the top of her head that wouldn't cede first place to Sedona.

"We are a working Warren. We are Witches, not researchers. Shifters from around the globe come to us for spells and guidance."

"Proper guidance requires knowledge!" Ash protested.

"It does. And in our off-time all of the Hares do, of course, continue their studies. Yet mundane research is *not* our focus. We are Hares. We are *Witches*."

"But…!"

"Stop." One word, one tired hand rising into the air, and all of Ash's arguments died away. "Ashbaline, you will never be welcome in my Warren. You're not a Hare. You're just Kin."

There it was. The bottom line. The fact that made her face burn with shame.

Only a handful of Shifters' children grew up to be Shifters themselves. Some Kinds, like Wolves, often bred true. Not Hares, though. At birth, Ash lost the Shifter genetic lottery. No matter how hard she studied, no matter how much she pushed herself, she would never be her mother's equal. She wasn't a Hare… so she wasn't a Witch.

End of story, to Mom.

Though not to her. "I may not be a full Witch, I admit. However I still believe that I've got some sensitivity, some psychic abilities that…"

"Stop." The command was sharper now, frustrated. "This is pathetic. If you had any useful magical skills, I would know."

'Pathetic.' Her cheeks burned as hot as the afternoon sun. That was what her own mother thought of her.

"You need to stop requesting admission to the Warren. You've become embarrassing."

Nausea swept over her, a shame so deep it twisted her guts.

"My Witch Queen was especially displeased to find that you stole my ID and used it to infiltrate the Warren. A crime that reflects badly on me, too. Oh, Ashbaline, what were you thinking?"

I thought that if I could get my thesis on Danielle LePierre's desk, she'd read it and then she'd see *how much I could contribute to the Sedona Warren.*

"You need to accept reality. You are not a Shifter. You will never be a Shifter – or the equal of a Shifter. Accept what you are."

A failure. Kin. A disappointment.

"Do you understand me? This ends, now. Agreed?"

"Yes." Her mouth said the words, as it had a dozen times before.

This time, however, even her heart couldn't disagree.

That cloud of gloom hovered over Ash all the way back to her apartment in downtown Phoenix. It stayed throughout the weekend, as she brooded about her future. What was the point of getting a Ph.D. now? Nothing she did would ever be good enough for her mother or the Warren.

On Monday night the phone rang. When she answered, a cheery woman's voice poked the first hole in her misery. "Hi, I'm trying to reach Ash Anderson."

"Speaking."

"Are you the author of 'Continuity of Liturgical Symbolism in Ancestral Pueblan Art'?"

"Yes…" Summer was a strange time to get a call from the university.

Delight bubbled around the caller's words, a contagious excitement that felt like a cool breeze on Ash's scorched soul. "Great! I'm Lucy Adams from the L.A. Warren."

Shock nearly made her drop the phone. A Hare… calling her? And from L.A. – a Warren every bit as good as Sedona! "How did you hear about my thesis?"

"One of the Hares in Sedona sent me a copy. It's… wait. You're Magdalene Anderson's daughter, right?"

"Yes."

"Good. So you're not going to flip out if I talk about Shifters."

"No, not at all," she said with a laugh.

"Whew! That's a relief. Well, as I was saying, I got a copy and thought your ideas were brilliant. They could be the breakthrough we need to understand what the rock art in this region truly means."

Each word enveloped her like a loving hug. A gentle kiss to whisk away all the pain of her bruises. "Thank you. Hearing that means… well, thank you."

"Of course! Though I have to ask an awkward question. Why didn't Sedona snap you up?"

Oh. That explained why she was calling. Ash's heart sank as Fate forced her to destroy her own chances. "I'm just Kin."

"Okay." The Hare paused, long enough to stir a confused hope. "And that keeps you out of their research cadre… why?"

"Research… what?"

"Research cadre. A body of academics, both mundane and Shifter, associated with a Warren. Focusing on specialized but non-magical projects that augment the Warren's magical work."

Holy crap! That had been her dream since she was a little girl…

CONTINUE READING THE NEXT STORY IN THE SHIFTERS OF THE Aegis, Damaged Lost Wolf, here on Amazon…